Tale of the Turk
Journey of a Soul

by

Sydney Prentice

Hermitage Press

Published by Hermitage Press
226 Cotorro Lane, Saint Augustine, Florida 32086
(904) 794-0248

Editor: Rosemary Heffernan
Book Design: Vera Doherty

Library of Congress Cataloging-in-Publication Data
98-71609
Prentice, Sydney
Tale of The Turk; Journey of a Soul by Sydney Prentice
ISBN 0-9666-998-0-7: $12.95
Printed in the United States of America

Contents

Illustrations

To...

All Seekers of the Light

1998

Acknowledgments

For the spark that ignited the publication of this book I am grateful to The Learning Channel's segment "Paleontologists" from their series "The Paleo World" hosted by Dr. Robert Bakker. Thanks to Elizabeth Hill, Historian at Carnegie Museum, who was delighted to hear from me then asked the question that ignited my effort. *"Was he (my father) also a writer? We have some of his notebooks."* My deep appreciation to Rosemary Heffernan, my editor, for computerizing my typed, cut and paste pages and for her infinite patience as we puzzled over obscure words and phrases. Thanks to Nancy Roca, photographer, for her skillful scanning and adapting some of my father's early published art works. For the book design, which incorporates the essenced of the story, I thank my long-time friend, Vera Doherty, graphic designer. For technical assistance on the project, the skills of Richard Kipper were a major contribution.

A SUMMER NIGHT
'Tis a night in June
And the crescent moon
Floats high
In the early evening sky.

The mighty marsh-land all at rest,
The moon's bright image in his breast,
Throws out upon the evening skies
His floating flaunting fire-flies.
Then the insect chorus sings
Of all the things
They find in their wild wanderings
Beneath the day-blue skies.
The marsh so silent all the day
Now gives his fettered fancies sway,
And to the silver moon he shows
A light that daylight never knows—
The dancing fire-fly light of June.
All this magic swarm that dances
Are but maddened, burning fancies
Of the marsh that loves the moon,
And the moonlight
Of the June night
Puts all his heart in tune.

Ah, now I know
Why his fancies glow,
And why the evening insects croon
Such a sweet enchanting song
While the dizzy dancing throng
Keeps time to the tune,
For the moon light
Of the June night
Is a love-smile from the moon.
SYDNEY PRENTICE

Sydney Prentice

About the Author

HE AUTHOR, Sydney Clark Prentice, was born May 14, 1871 in Washington, D.C. In 1876 his parents moved to Lawrence, Kansas, where Sydney grew up with seven younger brothers and three sisters. He was a nature lover and by the time he became a teenager he had filled notebooks with flowing, descriptive passages of his adventures with his friends. He enhanced his stories with skillful pencil drawings.

In 1896 he graduated from the University of Kansas with a Bachelor of Arts degree in Fine Arts. In 1900, a Master of Arts degree followed.

The classical curriculum of that time consisted of Latin, Greek, German, French, English Literature, Advanced Logic, Psychology, Metaphysics, Elocution, Philosophy, Drawing and Painting and English Composition.

Prentice became known for his "fanciful writings and charming illustrations... his artistry comes straight from elfland and transmutes all it touches." (*Graduate Magazine of Kansas University, November, 1914)*

He focused on his art work by enrolling in The Art Institute of Chicago. Then he began doing scientific drawings for the Field Museum in Chicago. This led to an invitation from Carnegie Museum in Pittsburgh to come and be their staff artist in paleontology. He remained there forty-five years, becoming an internationally recognized paleontological artist whose drawings of fossils are still studied by scientists today. He traveled frequently to the National Museum in Washington, D.C., and to the Museum of Natural History in New York to illustrate many of their unique fossils. One small fossil bears his name.

Fluent in French, he lectured at the Alliance Français in Pittsburgh. Other lectures in English concerned poets and their works.

He married a Scottish lass, Alice Henderson, in 1917. Their only child, Irene Prentice Allemano, now resides in St. Augustine, Florida.

Irene remembers her father writing in the evenings "a story," parts of which he read to her shortly before his unexpected transition in 1943.

He lives on in this story, a metaphysical life-quest adventure, as well in his extraordinarily accurate drawings of fossils. His photograph stands today at the entrance to Dinosaur Hall in Carnegie Museum in Pittsburgh.

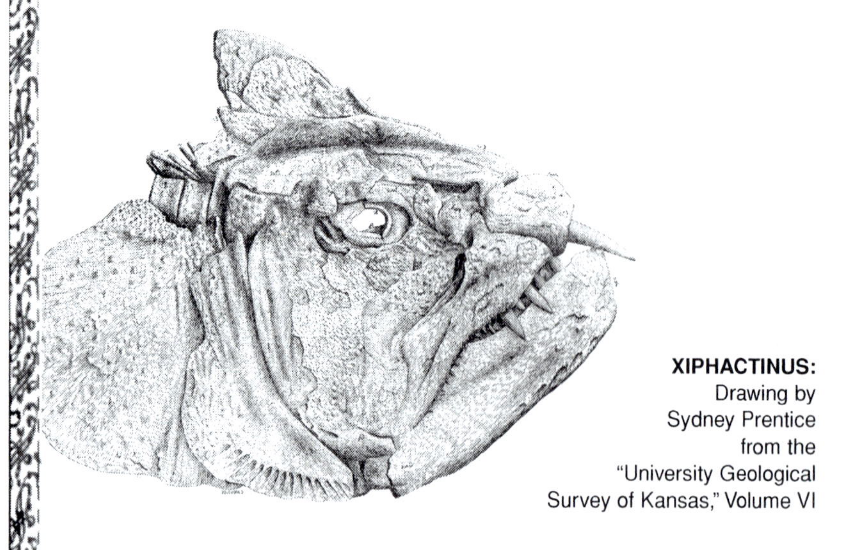

XIPHACTINUS: Drawing by Sydney Prentice from the "University Geological Survey of Kansas," Volume VI

Prologue

Birth Of A Story
How This Came To Be

Do You Believe In Synchronicity?

It was a Sunday evening in January 1995 when I returned home from a long day of varied activities. Thinking I might relax by watching a program about ancient history on the Learning Channel, I turned on the television, something I rarely do.

The screen lit up with a segment titled, *The Paleo World.* A scientist was talking about renowned paleontologists of the past. Photographs of these people were framed on the wall beside him. About to turn off the TV (I grew up in museums), I paused a moment when I recognized photographs of two of the scientists, one of whom visited my childhood home in Pittsburgh. Then the camera shifted and in the corner of the frame was my father looking at me from his photo!

He made his transition 55 years ago! Stunned! Cracks in dimensions opened up and I fell in. The past became present.

Where in this country could those photos be? Thus began a telephone journey that took me from Bozeman, Montana to Boulder, Colorado to Middleton, Connecticut to Pittsburgh, Pennsylvania.

In the process, I learned that his drawings of fossils are still being studied by scientists today.

"They are classics."

"His legacy is secured."

Those were among the comments about the work of my father from present day paleontologists I spoke with. Since I had no copies of his work, a call to the Carnegie Museum in Pittsburgh led to a gracious offer to send me a commemorative issue of his work. I was told that his photograph stands at the entrance to Dinosaur Hall. The museum also offered to send some of his notebooks.

"Was he a writer?" I was asked.

"Ah," I replied, *"I have his manuscript of a Grail quest story which has travelled with me through lives in nine different countries."*

At the time of my father's death, neither of us had a clue as to the long journeys I would be taking. Though I had begun transcribing his manuscript more than forty years ago, subsequent transfers to different countries intervened, presenting me with their challenging situations, some of them spine chilling.

I had abandoned the project.

I remembered my father once saying to me, *"Irene, someday you will finish this."*

I had no idea what he meant.

Well, the universe said, *"Now is the time."* Fifty-five years ago I did not understand the answers to the three quest questions. I learned about the third one, The Philosopher's Stone, while living in Argentina. It was there that the mystery unfolded for me while studying books on alchemy! This discovery took place just before returning to my native country, America.

Imagine my surprise when I discovered, in reading my father's manuscript, that the timing is the same for Ali the Weaver, whom you will soon meet in *Tale of the Turk.*

Ali, too, makes his discovery just prior to returning to his native country!

I translated the alchemical process into an art work done in the ancient traditional Spanish medium known as *estofado.* This is an icon-like process applied to wood with many undercoatings upon which is laid 23 K gold. This is followed by burnishing, chiseling and finally oil painting.

In 1986 I created such a work entitled, *The Seeker,* depicting a person holding a symbol of the Philospher's Stone while standing in the refining fires of life's experiences. It was exhibited in six major cities having been one of 40 winners selected out of 11,000 entries in an art competition sponsored by *Modern Maturity* magazine.

It is my biography. It is every seeker's biography.

As I transcribed my father's hand-lettered writings, an amazing revelation began to unfold. I was reading a prophetic story of my own life's journey.

It is with love and gratitude for the inspiration my father gave to me that I now offer his/our story to the public. Maybe you, the reader, will find it to be your story, too.

— Irene Prentice Allemano
The Hermitage
February, 1998

"Si tu n'étreins que des chimères,
si tu bois L'enivrement des vins illusoires, qu'importe!
Le soleil meurt, la foule imaginaire est morte
Mais le monde subsiste en ta seul âme; vois!
Les jours sont fanées comme des roses brèves.
Mai ton Verbe a créé le mirage où tu vis."

— Pierre Quillard
Book of Masques by
Remi de Gourmont

"If you clasp only chimera, if you drink the intoxication of delusive wine, what matter! The sun dies, the imaginary crowd is dead, but the world subsists in your soul. See! The days are faded like brief roses, but your Word has created the mirage in which you live."

— Pierre Quillard

"The land of Chimera is the only one in the world that is worth dwelling in ... There is nothing beautiful except that which does not exist."

— Rosseau

"Unashamed to be sublimely ridiculous and ridiculously sublime."

— Duncan Phillips

"The best part of you is the rainbow in your mind. You need enchantment. Life is cold and dead without fairies and ogres. Little children who are familiar with such unrealities are the happiest portion of the race."

— Dr. Frank Crane

Prelude

"The quarrels of love are the beginning of love."

—Terrence

Bernie! Come here to this window. See this Arabian night!"

I made not the slightest response.

Sam resumed, *"A full round moon of rose carnelian is set in a sky of turquoise and lapis-lazuli. The fish pond in the garden has taken the moon into its turquoise heart, and the willows round the pond bend down to the mirrored moon with their tresses intertwined with moonbeams. Beyond the pond the nervous poplars in a row sway and swoon like slim-waisted girls all ready to dance under the blue dome of a Sultan's palace. Come see this show."*

Receiving no answer, he added, *"Then listen to the music of the night. Hear those katydids singing in the shadow caves of the elm trees, and the crickets chirring in the thickets. Tree frogs answer from the branches, and a screech owl twitters with it all. Hear the insect orchestration for this blue-green, moonlit night of perfume. The whole ensemble is like a prelude to some new tale of Scheherazade."*

He paused for a moment of contemplation, then he concluded, *"Ominous night! Oracular night! Night of nodding moon-kissed trees! Bernard Sylvester, wake up! Here's the night before your birthday."*

I was in no emotional mood to be enkindled by this flight of fancy from the mind of Samuel Simpson. I was quite accustomed to such sudden outpourings. For during the whole summer he felt inspired to create what he called Polyphonic Rhythms in which he imitated the sounds and interpreted the meanings of the various voices of nature. So I let him stand there all unanswered at an open window of this large room where no evening lamp had yet been lighted. My mind was somber with forebodings because I felt convinced that Samuel and I must give up our nights of moon-gazing as well as our days of meadow-rambling and we must go to work at once and earn our income.

This morning's mail delivered two disquietous letters. The one to Samuel was from the girl who had recently broken her engagement of marriage with him; the letter to me offered each of us a promising position in a corporation newly organized in the enterprising city of Kanopolis located just over the state line and about an hour's train ride from our town. It was up to us to accept these positions now or never. I expected Samuel's opposition to this offer, so I tactfully allowed him to stand there at the window where he was crooning with the insect orchestration of this warm midcontinental night in the month of August in a year at the turn of the century. During all this irksome evening I had been sitting in this room alert for the favorable moments in which to broach to Samuel this letter from genial Hecktor Byng, or Judge Byng as he was commonly called.

At length abruptly Sam called out, *"Are you asleep Bernard"?*

A grunt of negation was my sole reply.

"You say you never saw the Maid of the Moon. Distinctly you could see her now. She was never so lovely before."

"My eyes are for realities."

"Radiantly real is the Moon Girl tonight with her head tossed back for a kiss from the Man in the Moon."

"No moon-folks for me tonight, Sam."

"Then please hold your tongue 'til I ask you to speak again."

In complete compliance I slumped back into the patient silence which I had maintained since the darkening of the daylight. The nightfall penetrated my soul and unleashed presentments which were even more somber, and into my mind stalked obscure fears like black panthers abroad in a fearsome forest. Broodingly I sat there, swallowed up in darkness, on the oriental divan in the center of this large high-ceilinged room.

In recoil from fears of the future and frustrations of the present my mind fled to memories of my father, whom I loved with all my soul. I recalled how oft he had admonished me to hold fast to these three precious things: the first is gentleness; the second is economy; and the third is humility. From childhood I had been somewhat solitary and over cautious almost to the verge of cowardice. My young mother died on the day of my birth. She was a half-sister to the mother of Samuel and so it came about, after the death of my father, that I was installed in the cheerful home of the Simpsons where I grew up with Samuel, their only child. We were comrades in boyish sports and classmates in college.

Vividly now I recalled these last words which Samuel's father addressed to me, "I sometimes fear that too much moonlight and music has filtered into the brain of my boy. My dear Bernard, I am leaving his fate to your prudence and practical sense. As soon as you two boys are through with college I want you to get Sam into a business career."

Uncle Dexter was in the room at the time and he

joined our discourse. This was the day before the father and mother and uncle set forth on that fatal round-the-world voyage on the private yacht in which Uncle Dexter owned a good-sized share. Samuel's mother took a chair in our circle just in time to hear Uncle Dex remark, *"Yes, Sam would be a bully boy in business. I want to make him a partner and a manager in my chain of tempermental restaurants."*

Dex was a lawyer by profession, but in personality, he was a man of fads and fancies. He delighted in concocting salads and novel dishes for the pleasure of his dinner guests, and partly out of sport, he had founded, in different cities, a chain of so-called temperamental restaurants, each one with a cognomen fitted to its gastronomic atmosphere, to wit: the Saucisserie suggested a super-sauce and a sausage: the Sorcerie was more of a woman's cafe in which a gipsy girl read the palms of those who cared to lend a hand; there was the Snackerie for a snack; and a Chitchaterie for afternoon gossip; and last of all was the Pixy Puff, named after an imported mushroom.

During all this debate as to how Sam might be the manager of a chain of fancy restaurants, his mother looked on with noncommittal silence. When we looked to her for comment she turned her large appealing eyes directly into mine as she began, *"He has immense imagination"* ....

She would have said more but just at that moment Samuel himself strode into the room. Immediately a maid served the usual afternoon tea.

Early on the following day the parents and uncle set out on a journey from which they never returned. All three went down with the yacht in a typhoon off the Malayan coast.

This stroke of tragedy left Samuel the sole inheritor of these ample grounds and this old rambling house stored with all kinds of collections – books, engravings, stuffed game fish and birds, mounted heads of large animals, costumes and bibelots and jew-jaws and gadgets galore. Most of these things had been accumulated by Dexter Pendleton while touring and hunting in distant lands.

Of what earthly use could this museum of playthings be to Samuel Simpson today? There before me now his shadow stood at the window. My beloved Samuel; one of the town's most popular boys; my sublime, my comical Samuel; a marvelous mixture of contrarities; egotistic, fanciful, farcical, fond of good dinners, and like his Uncle Dexter, possessed of high spirits and long windedness. Samuel was genuine in music. He poured out his imaginative whimsies in reams and streams of verses , some of which were rather good but most of which were very bad. But whenever he set a verse to music his melody redeemed the doggerel. Small wonder that Samuel took to music. A grandfather played the violincello, his mother was a singer and played the piano and his father played the trombone. At the age of nineteen Sam had written an orchestral composition which though puerile, was of promise. At the age of twenty-two, he was the drum major of the brass band of our town, an office in which he still took great pride.

Yes, Samuel had immense imagination. He might compose a worthy symphony in due time. Recalling the mother's appealing eyes, I resolved at this moment not to interrupt his flight of fancies at the window. During this whole hot day I had endured Sam's froth and fury over the final goodbye-for-good letter which came in the morning. I say final letter because there had been more than one goodbye letter during the summer. However, Samuel declared this one to be the "utmost of all finality." Phoebe West. He might have married Phoebe last June had not a lover's quarrel intervened. Silly quarrel it was, but it broke their engagement. What a long day this had seemed to me! When it came time for the evening meal I had not been able to read Byng's letter to Sam. After supper we retired to the seclusion of this library room. Then Sam insisted on more readings from the goodbye epistle. He read and re-read each page and paragraph and with so many discursive comments that the daylight played out before he was through. Then for a whole hour we had kept lounging here in the library with not a word between us. By the end of that hour a velvet blackness had obliterated every object in the room except the ruby flaunting spark of Sam's cigar. When the cigar was finished Sam went to the window to breathe the fresh air, and that was the moment when Sam had summoned me to meet the Maid of the Moon, and when my noncompliance had brought upon me his demand that I keep silent.

I was still maintaining that obligatory silence sprawled on the cushions contemplating Samuel and wondering what he would do next. He lit a fresh cigar - one of those very long and expensive cigars which Uncle Dexter used to order directly from Havana. Sam was so enamoured with this excellent aroma that he supported this special order, but reserved the smoking of this choice cigar for his moments of inspiration. From this I surmised he felt a fit of inspiration coming on; therefore I refrained from speech and watched his comic capers at the window.

There stood the shadow-form of Samuel in silent silhouette conducting an imaginary orchestra with a ruby-tipped cigar. He had gone through such antics during the whole of this summer, translating and mimicking songs of katydids and crickets and grasshoppers and cicadas, to say nothing of the bird songs. To all those tuneful lyrics he gave the name of Midget Madrigals. To me all this seemed but an amusing drollery, but to Sam it was the serious creation of a new kind of lyric verse.

Then I fell to wondering how came it about that Samuel Simpson, the fire-minded impulsivist, could have fallen into love for Phoebe West, a girl of planetary composure and who, in other respects was an exact complement of Samuel. Her classic face, her great brown enquiring eyes, her irresistible smile made her an adorable girl. On occasion she could be the life of the party with her wit and humor. Small wonder that she was the most promising graduate of her class in a New England Seminary. Perhaps she understood Samuel better than he knew; and perhaps in her heart she may have a latent vanity that was fed by the vociferous love-pangs of this strapping fellow. To me it was strange and sad that Sam's brilliant courtship with this beautiful girl should have crashed on that fatal quarrel of not so long ago. Now the whole affair seemed wrecked beyond repair. So what to do? To me it seemed, that after a whole summer of emotional uncontrol, it was surely time for Samuel Simpson to rise from the wreck and start life all over again.

On the sill of the window lay the letter from Phoebe just where Sam had put it down when the daylight failed. It was indeed a longish letter, a veritable dissertation, written in violet ink on single sheets of lavender paper. The awakening night-breeze lifted these pages and dropped them in the darkness, one by one, like the petals of a rose that is blown. On the carpet wavered uneasy flecks of moonlight which had sifted through the spray of ivy just outside the window, and into these moon-dapples an occasional page of Phoebe's letter fell.

A chapter in the life of Samuel Simpson was at an end. And what would his choice of a new chapter be? Would he keep up his rhyming of dreams into song? Would he turn his imaginations to writing exotic menus for temperamental restaurants? Or would he lend his hands to practical common sense work in a new construction plant which was sure of a great future?

A scent of tuberose and of petunia and of moon-flower came in from the gardens, and as these fragrances flowed over Samuel they took on a tinge of his Havana, blending into a distinctive incense for this particular evening. The night breeze came in stronger now, so to hold Byng's letter on the table I weighted it down with the yellow brick which was a sample of the product that was soon to be put on the market.

Here Samuel broke his long spell of silence, *"Those katydids! Hear them! Those mad – those mischievous midgets – telling all the tribes of night that Phoebe West has thrown Sam Simpson down! Now Bernie! You just keep still while I catch the motif of this madrigal."*

He seemed in much emotion as he hearkened to this insect madrigal. He kept crooning softly to himself meanwhile. For a moment the enchantment of the evening took hold upon my suppressed fancy; for a moment I seemed to hear a meaning in the cheeping of the katydids. I seemed to hear this meaning more distinctly when Samuel in clear and steady voice declaimed:

Phoebe did! She did!
She jilted me!
She sweetly neatly cheated me!
She did! Phoebe did!

From tree to tree far and near came the antiphonal of the katydids:

She did!
Phoebe did!

Samuel responded:

She said she'd wed.
Phoebe did.
She cut me dead
Instead!
Said my head was dense as lead!
Said it red!

Phoebe did!

Antiphonal of katydids:

So she did!
Phoebe did!

Samuel turned halfway from the window to declare:

I vow revenge for what she did!
I'll lift my name to fame amid
The highest stars of heaven's head
And make her sorry that she said
What she did!

Then Samuel, eagerly attentive, stood with hands on the sill, leaning far out of the window and, as I imagined, trying to hear what the katydids might say to that.

My patience played out. I switched on the lamps. A gleam shot into the trees before the window and hushed the katydids. Slowly Sam drew in his head, turned around, stared open-mouthed at me and he said, *"I requested you to keep still. Do you know what you have done? You have...."*

"Enough of the Maid in the Moon! Sam! The heat of the day and that letter from Phoebe have made away with your reason. Now in this flag-end of the day let us focus our common sense on a hard reality – the brick proposition."

As though he heard not a word of mine he went on, *"Bernard Sylvester! You have stabbed the climax of the music of this night. You have driven from my mind the PRELUDE to my Song of Songs."*

"Plain duty. I promised your father...."

Still ignoring me he continued, *"The nuance of the night was singing itself into my brain just when your electric searchlight stabbed into those moon-kissed trees. Now give me a breathing spell to recapture that run-away motif of moonlight."*

In feverish endeavor Sam kept repeating some meaningless musical syllables. Finally he shook his head despairingly and took to pacing the floor and pressing his wrists to his temples in an attitude of feigned agony. *"You murdered my PRELUDE, my aria of the crooning nodding trees and the moon-kissed pond and the sweet melancholy of tuberose."*

"Come down from the tree-tops Samuel!"

"O Bernie, the poet, Samuel Coleridge, could never recall the ending for his Kubla Kahn after he had been slam-banged in the midst of the recording of his vision! Ah me! How did it go? Heigh ho, trolollie tollie low. Heigh lo lo. No! That was not the melody!" He smothered his face in his hands and went stumbling across the room. *"That PRELUDE! It kissed me for a moment. Now it's lost forever!"*

"Wake out of your sleep walk! Rub open your eyes and look at some hard realities. Do you hear anything I am saying?"

"You are always a hurdle in my path whenever I start for the stars."

"Leave the moon and the stars in heaven where they belong. There is a very earthly thing for our consideration right here and now. You hear me?"

"I was born on the birthday of Napoleon and under the stars of Leo – born when the sun was a guest of the Lion."

"Harping obsolete astrology to an era of applied mechanics," I replied.

"Caesar relied on his Stars of the Lion. So did Napoleon. So why not I? Bernie, your birthday comes under the Sign of Virgo. You will always be a peaceful passive soul – a sort of an astral Lamb. I shall always be an astral Lion."

"Astral Ass, you better say."

Disdaining further comment I took up Byng's letter in one hand and the sample brick in the other, then I called out. *"Tonight! Now! This means a yes or a no. Right now!"*

"You have a letter. Yes. Right now. Yes. I saw it in the morning mail addressed in the Honorable Judge Byng's hand scrawl. Now put down that brick and hold off Byng's blurb for awhile. I am not through with all my letter reading and I have the stage just now."

"Will you ever come to the end of your letters?"

"The daylight played out before I got to this one."

"And the daylight will return before you are through. Very well then. Your letter. Snap it out promptly."

Maintaining self-restraint I replaced the brick on the letter from Byng.

In considerate tone Sam said, *"I was all through with Phoebe's letter when the sun went down. While the darkness was coming on I sat in yonder corner silently speculating as to what that letter really meant. It implied more than it expressed; and Phoebe has an art of innuendo, as you know.*

"I read that letter twice before its innuendo dawned on me, and I shall have to read it all again when my mind clears to more clairvoyance. But here is a letter from her Aunt Drucilla expressed in cannon shots. It follows Phoebe's flare of lightning like a thunder clap."

"Well hurry the night shift of reading. Then allow me to read of an opportunity which knocks but once in a ...."

"Knocks but once! Egad! Since last June this brick-bat opportunity of Byng's has been knocking like a riveting hammer. Throttle that hammer for awhile. Drucilla Burby has some knocking now."

"Let us hear then what she knocks."

Sam interjected, *"Drucilla Burby! Fat, forty and furious! Unmarriageable, unmanageable, tyrannical guardian of her sister's orphaned child, the lovely Phoebe West. Phoebe's aunt. She's related to our Simpson family only through a marriage as you well know. She has chastised me all my life; therefore she considers it her prerogative to deliver to me now this masterpiece of verbal invective."*

"Since all is now ended between you and Phoebe, what matters a letter from Drucilla now?"

"Well this letter is an elucidation of Phoebe's innuendo, an affirmation of what Phoebe artfully implies. While Drucilla was writing this letter I can imagine how her desk must have shivered and shaken under the stabs of her pen which actually cut into the paper. I can imagine how she read all this to Phoebe and how Phoebe's angelic voice said, "Amen." I can see Drucilla's big fat fist pounding this stamp on the letter."

"Don't poison your mind with false imaginations."

"Drucilla's letter leaves no margins for imagined meanings."

"Let me hear then what she says."

"First let me collect Phoebe's letter from the floor before you tramp upon it. See how the breeze has scattered her pages! And such a lot of them! She spent a whole day in writing those pages; I'm sure that she did. There lies one under the book case, and two under the divan, and look, yonder lies one which has floated under the far end of the grand piano." Sam began harvesting the pages. When he crawled from under the piano, with the errant page in his teeth, he sat upright on the carpet for a moment to puff and perspire and arrange the pages in consecutive order. When that was done he still sat there and fixing his big blue eyes upon me he said, *"Would you believe it" Drucilla in her letter called me straight out Humpty Dumpty."*

I always had to laugh when someone called him Humpty Dumpty, but in this moment he was in such a comic pose that I laughed to tears. Sam glowered. Then he placed the pages on the carpet, lighted a cigar and prepared to sit there 'til I laughed it out.

How did it happen that Samuel gained the nickname of Humpty Dumpty? Way back in high-school days Sam composed a pantomime entitled, "Sir Humpty Dumpty", and in which he played the role of Humpty on a little stage of the third floor of his home where his audience of classmates filled every available seat. So clever were the skits and antics of Sam in this show that his friends often called him Humpty Dumpty, after that or just Humpty for short. After a while he soured on this nickname but he could not shake if off. This amateur theater of Samuel's was equipped with footlights, stage and scenery and curtain, all of which came into Samuel's hands after his Uncle Dexter replaced the little worn-out playhouse of the town with a modern structure. Thus Samuel suddenly found himself a stage manager, an actor and a dramatic composer all in one. He promptly organized an amateur dramatic club which he called the Heliconians. This name was suggested by the drop curtain's adorable painting of Apollo and the Muses in their dwelling place on Mount Helicon. For his performances Samuel availed himself of Uncle Dexter's valuable collections of old oriental costumes from which he borrowed that most valuable garment of all, the magnificent turban and toggery which he wore in his title role of Ali Baba. I suspect that Samuel wrote that play in order to strut around in that fabulous silk and velvet gown. It inflated his imagination to parade in costume. During his college years Sam presented a version of The Frogs of Aristophanes in which his frog chorus with its brekekekex, koax, koax, was the hit of the evening.

The advent of this little stage in the Simpson home profoundly affected the life of Samuel. It awoke in him a flair of dramatic phantasmagoria which clung to him the remainder of his days, and it explains his propensity to drop into histrionic speech and pose and commonplace occasions.

Samuel, still seated on the carpet of the library resumed, *"So Drucilla and Phoebe and their ally, that squirrel-mouthed Polliver Paul, have Humpty-Dumptified me in the ears of this town. Polliver tells them my lyric songs are composed of bug-buzzings and frog-croakings. To this day he pokes fun at my frog chorus. Brekekekex! But that is not all. With more ingenuity Polliver has dubbed me Simp Sampson. That started a hee-haw that is still going the rounds."*

"A rival is always ready with ridicule."

"A rival! Pooh! Polliver! Koax! But after all how can I have a rival when I'm all through with Phoebe? He tells Phoebe that the little philosophical book she wrote lit up his lonely life. Ha, he. That darksome doleful life of his! He thinks his self-abasement may melt the pitying heart of Phoebe to love. But women are not won by the weakness, especially the self-sufficient Phoebe West."

"Yes, rivals ridicule. But make an end of this prattle of Paul. He does not concern us now."

Sam persisted, *"Polliver says my verses are great in sound and unsound in sense – says they are brilliant phrases with no theme – gay feathers without a bird – a skin without a skeleton. Polliver once tried his hand at stuffing birds, you know. He says I have more words than wisdom."*

"Why do you call him Polliver while his real name is Oliver?"

"Because he is a Polliver. That is the name I gave to the mutton-head character in the cleverest bit of melodrama I ever wrote."

"Don't make him out a villain, Sam."

"He'll always be just a Polliver to me."

Sam got up from the floor, shook himself into shape, put away Phoebe's letter. Then he said, *"Before I read the letter from Drucilla I wish to recall some past occurrences to your mind."*

"Now don't go back to the past! Let us look to the future."

"Well perhaps you may recall that letter from Phoebe which said my mind was dense as an apple dumpling."

"O Humpty! Don't dig up that dumpling epithet any more It was only in retaliation to your inability to see any meaning in the little book she wrote about the apple tree. It made you mad. Then she took it back and wrote instead your head was dense as lead. I remember how that downed you."

"Downed me? Did it? No! It didn't! Now let me explain what I am driving at just now. That 'dense as lead' of hers hit me like a bullet, but it released in my mind some creative powers I never dreamed I had. In about an hour I penned my keenest bit of satire in reply – all in verse and rhyme – and mailed it to her post haste in Special Delivery right away."

"I remember that whirligig of windy words."

"Very well. Have your sarcasm. But this final letter from Phoebe has unsealed a well of inspiration in my mind. It has released in me such creative powers as I never dreamed I had. I hear new strains of music pressing to be played and now lyrics urging to be sung. I feel stung to action, and for this new birth of mine thanks be to Phoebe West and Aunt Drucilla."

Laughingly I rejoined, *"Samuel Simpson! Prince of Pother! All your burlesque would make a bully book if you would jot it down and name that book 'The Dumptiad'."*

He paused in his fury, mopped his brow, relaxed his face into a smile. *"Egad! I feel I could put through even a book like that. The Dumptiad! Sure! Something in the spirit of Pope's Dunciad! I will write up every dunderhead I know. Drucilla Burby done in burlesque. Ah! Ha! Ha!*

Hillebrand and Byng and you, too, Child of Virgo. I shall feature Polliver Paul, atrabillious Polliver Paul, with his face of a squirrel and eyes of a fish, and with neckties grey as a buckwheat cake. Right now I can see the patterns for these skits clearly cut as cameos. I shall write them all up to a tune as nimble as the music of a merry-go-round."

I turned away from this talkativeness and sauntered round the room. I stopped before a colored portrait of Napoleon on the wall. To assuage the flow of Sam's tempestuous speech I remarked, *"Uncle Dex was right. You do look like this picture."*

Sam made no response. Again I interjected, *"Why do you fuss and fume any longer about Phoebe and her book? There's a lot of big fish in the sea."*

"Big fish! I don't want Phoebe back! Nevermore Phoebe! She and I belong to antagonistic constellations. I only want to make her sorry for the words she wrote to me, and I want her to know my mind is more of lightning than of lead."

"With your Napoleonic face and your witty-worded mind you could be a lion among the ladies. This very day you received an invitation to where dwells the finest and prettiest girl in town."

With depreciating voice Sam replied, *"Bernard, your looks are better than mine – hair thick and curly – face femininely fine – innocent large brown eyes – a chin well formed and dimpled but somewhat narrow like those born under Virgo. Many a girl will fall for such as you. Go yourself to that big man's home and marry his pretty little daughter. As for me, Bernard, I am the kind that loves but one and loves but once. So now I am through with love."*

"Well, Sam there is more to life than just being married. Look at Uncle Dex. He lived happily enough, it seems."

"Uncle Dex let woman alone. He was never so stung by waspish females as have I. Phoebe and Drucilla have this day challenged my intelligence. Now I shall write a volume that will put Phoebe's book in the shade."

"Don't grow too bookish, Sam. Bookish men are bores. Talk more about baseball and race tracks and boxing bouts just as you and Uncle Dexter used to do. Happy bachelor! I never heard him whimper over women."

"Books! My father and his father devoured books. My mother was a writer. Dexter could have been another Balzac had he tried. My people have fed on miles and miles of literature."

Here Sam wafted his arm toward the crowded shelves.

"It's in my blood that stuff that books are made of. I am planning now a book which the authoress of the Apple Tree will never dub an apple dumpling.

"Sam! Sam! Draw the bit on your run-away mind! Where is that letter from Drucilla?!

"Right here. How you heckle me tonight! Here's the letter. Listen to this."

But just at that moment the unexpected happened. Into the room came the old man-servant, Casper, slow-walking on silent feet, solemn as an undertaker, serious as a priest.

Casper, the deaf mute who had served as handyman to Uncle Dex ever since Samuel was a small child. On a silver platter he bore a bulbous pitcher clinking with lumps of ice in a dark-hued beverage with green leaves of mint in its make-up. There were also some dainty little sandwiches of cheese and caviar and thin-sliced meats. There were olives and little cakes. On the tray was a placard inscribed in Casper's best handwriting:

Greetings to Bernard on his birthday
which comes in at midnight,
and
here is a special punch
and a special bit of lunch
from Casper.

In glad surprise Sam clasped his hands together and exclaimed with a smile on his face, *"A delicious drink for a sweltering night!"*

Said I, *"A grateful intermission in our heated disputations."*

Casper bowed and smiled and grasped my hand and then took silent leave. He was square-faced, smooth-shaven, small-eyed, and bald as a door knob. His sagging cheeks hung round his mouth like the jowls of a mastiff dog. He always carried a pencil and pad but he was miraculously adept in lip-reading, and he was able to communicate with Samuel and me through a code of gestures and facial grimaces.

"What's in that punch, Sam?"

"There you go, as usual; obstinate, obdurate, always objecting." Sam lifted a well-filled glass. "Here's to a new birthday of Bernard Sylvester. May his stars greet him with good fortune on this day!"

I found my birthday punch was indeed a grateful draught. Sam filled a second glass from which he sipped more leisurely. Between sips he said, *"For the moment let us briefly review the program of your birthday breakfast."*

I knew full well that these preparations were not primarily for my birthday. Sam made this occasion an excuse to assemble in his home some of his fantastic friends before whom he could show off in reciting his latest verses.

"We shall have five guests, each one a specialist in his line. Five!" Sam held up his outstretched palm in emphasis, and while counting his fingers he continued, *"First is our thunder-thoughted poet friend, Cornelius Hillebrand, a Heliconian, who will recite his latest poems. Our second guest is Compton Daniels, the hunch-back. You've met him here. He's now a solicitor for that new futuristic publishing house in Kanopolis. If he likes our poems he may recommend our book for publication – Brand's and mine. He is a genius, a savant. But you will like him – that I know. The third guest is our Heliconian friend, young Emery Pendleton, Uncle Dexter's nephew, who is now a promising architect, and who will exhibit a plaster model of a café projected by Uncle Dex. The fourth guest is our old family friend, Marco Polo, as we dub him; and the fifth is our old chemical classmate, Jerry Coleman, who will demonstrate a new order of perfumes."*

"Wherefore perfumes, Sam?"

"You will hear of that later on. There will be some olfactory presentations at your birthday feast tomorrow. And Brand will have delicious verses about the powers of perfume."

"Firebrand Hillebrand! Pagan! Iconoclast! Socialist!"

"Heliconian Hillebrand! A new voice at this turn of the century – at this end of a prudish age! Promethian Hillebrand! Ravisher of Olympian fires!"

"You are risking your reputation in dining such as Hillebrand!"

"That was said of Emerson when he dined Walt Whitman."

"Hillebrand's writings corrupt young minds."

"And that was said of Socrates."

"Brand's social theories frighten the good and conservative folks."

"Bernard Sylvester! Your father was a clergyman, a worthy and an upright man, but steeped in the lore of the pre-scientific age. You associate with nice, negative, neutral men. You never swear or smoke or drink, and a dainty dinner has no more worth to you than to an alligator. Well and good! But you and I belong to different constellations. You approve of a milk-sop such as Polliver. I prefer the likes of Hillebrand. He was born under the stars of Taurus. Hillebrand! With the blood of a bull in his veins!"

"If Brand recites any more of those poems of nudity tomorrow, I leave the table."

"O Saint Sylvester! O Saint Anthony! Saint Anthony Comestock! Truth and art to you must be masked and fig-leaved. Your ears are dense as lead to katydids and your eyes are dumplings when it comes to seeing the Maid of the Moon! The nude is truth to Hillebrand; to you it suggests the Police Gazette. Brand is a literary genius who, like Walt Whitman, has gone native. He is a liberation to this over prudish, over costumed era."

"What more have you to say of my birthday breakfast?"

"Compton Daniels will have a lot to say. He is planning the make up of our book – the style of print and paper – ribbed paper, deckel-edged and sulphur-colored. Daniels is a man of exceptional good taste. He was tea taster and a wine taster, and an appraiser of perfumes and tobacco. He discovered and recommended those long and rare cigars for Uncle Dexter. And by the way, he is going to fit a perfume to my personality. That's one of his specialties – particular odors for particular personalities."

"Perfume for your personality?"

"Exactly. A perfume masculine but unobtrusive, a pungency subtle and restrained, but which dilates the

imagination – on odor which nobody else is able to obtain."

"Perfume! And at the very hour you should be choosing a job. You flabbergast me, Sam."

"Of course. And the paper which my poems are to be printed on must have that same subtle odor."

"Why Sam, this is sheer burlesque. This is copy fit for your Dumptiad. What ever put that notion in your head? Perfumed paper!"

"You ought to know by now that any perfume to Aunt Drucilla is as water to a mad dog. So this is just a clever item of my sweet revenge on her."

"You would be willing to praise the devil just because Drucilla hates him. Are you going to let that beady-eyed, fox-faced hunchback dab you and your book with perfume just to bedevil Drucilla? Sam, this is maddening."

"Brand approves of perfumed paper."

"Who ever heard of a perfumed book?"

"Why Bernard Sylvester! There lies one right before your eyes! Is your nose so dead that it never detected the fragrance of those pages?"

Sam took up Phoebe's book from the table, opened the covers, and thumb flipped the pages close to my face.

"Sniff that. What odor do you detect?"

"The pleasing smell of a new book "

"Smell! You could not smell a rat right under your nose. Well that's the perfume of apple blossoms. Compton Daniels told me that it might be a faint odor of prussic acid contained in the fiber of the paper. It must have been a happy accident. Drucilla would never approve of a perfumed book. Never. But that lucky accident gives a bright idea to me. When you open the pages of my new book a gale of joy will greet you."

"A grossly vulgar idea it seems to me."

"Of course! To you!"

Sam tossed the book back to the table. He poured himself more punch and while he sipped in little sips he stared over the rim of his glass at the little book lying there. It was in a snuff-colored binding of soft leather stamped with a gold design of a conventional tree with seven branches each of which bore seven golden apples. The title of the book was THE APPLE TREE. Each of the seven chapters contained seven little essays by Phoebe West and the chapters were cleverly interspersed with aphorisms, verses and parables culled from authors of early New England. The motif of the apple tree ran through all the chapters, beginning with the Tree of Knowledge in Eden and closing with the Tree of Life in Revelations. Of course The Book of Genesis does not say it was an apple tree, but that made no difference to Phoebe or Drucilla. At all events most people believe it was an apple tree.

Sam resumed, *"You may not like the hunchback but you will take to Emery Pendleton. He has grown to quite an architect by now. Dexter gave him the problem of designing the Pixy Puff café. He brings the completed plaster model here tomorrow. As to our good old friend, Marco Polo, he will suggest some oriental names for the new exotic dishes in our restaurants. He is going to tell us how, in Paris, they are now adding certain spicy aromas to portions of food."*

"Great Scott! Does he advocate perfumed food?"

"I calculated such an item would jar Drucilla's Puritanism so I want to get it into the newspaper that Marco is planning new savors for old foods."

We dubbed him Marco Polo because he had traveled far in oriental lands. He was born in Syria and his name was almost unpronounceable. He belonged to a syndicate which imported fancy comestibles such as marmalades, preserved fruits and sea foods, caviars, shoots of palm trees preserved in tin, honey from

Hymettus, and strange condiments and sauces. This syndicate dealt also in ancient and modern jewelry and in all kinds of curios and gadgets and relics from the remains of long forgotten cultures. Marco Polo found in Dexter Pendleton a good customer for his wares and he had supplied many an item for Dexter's Trophy Room and for his chain of restaurants.

Sam talked awhile on Marco's merits then he said, *"And the fifth fellow will be Jerry Coleman. You know Jerry."*

"Oh that comical chemical man – wiggles his ears – bats his eyes – stammers and stutters. What stunt will Jerry, the chemist, do?"

"Jerry, the alchemist, you better say. Perhaps you remember the day when I introduced him to Marco in this very room, and how Marco got him a job in a perfume laboratory. At that time Jerry was only an assistant instructor in chemistry – a starveling on a stipend. Look at him now. He will soon have money to burn. He runs the synthetic end of Marco's laboratories – makes perfumes out of coal tar or out of most any kind of plant juice. I may go into partnership with him and make perfumes. That would be another fragrant item of my revenge on Drucilla. My revenge on Phoebe shall be a more genteel affair. I propose to publish a book which shall be a three-ringed circus beside her little side show."

"The ignominy of all this talk."

"Very well, Bernard, I am much refreshed by your birthday punch. Now the next thing on our program shall be that letter from Drucilla."

Samuel held the letter with both hands and slowly, in a serious and monotonous tone, he read from the long invective epistle until he came to the final page. He handed this to me.

"There. Read with your own eyes this final thrust which Drucilla wrote in angry scrawl."

I read the paragraph he indicated but failed to grasp the meaning.

"What the deuce does she mean by declaring that you are 'a signal example of the Single Step'?"

"I knew that would stump your mind. The meaning of that lightning in the fog is this: I am the Single Step from the Sublime to the Ridiculous."

I gave way to a loud laugh.

"Laugh you dumpling. This may sound funny to you, but for me, Drucilla and Phoebe have hoodooed the initials of my name. After this they stand for Single Step. There's my full name all written out."

Sam tossed me his new straw hat. On the satin lining of the crown I saw the two golden initials of his name to which Sam had added in pencil additional letters to spell: Single Step.

"So that is the brand of the new name which I must endure until I am avenged of Drucilla's Single Step and Polliver's Simp Sampson."

Calmly Samuel lighted a fresh cigar. Then he rubbed his palms together and with histrionic grandiloquence he paced the floor.

"Now for a purple revenge! Mr. Single Step now steps forth to redeem his name – to outdo all those acid Calvinistic sayings that Drucilla hurled at me. She turned Phoebe dead against me with that old book of hers called Precepts of the Puritans, which to me is but a Dictionary of Don'ts. Phoebe culled a lot of sayings from that book. I shall answer all that sour-apple philosophy with a gale of joy. I shall answer it in the spirit of Hillebrand's neopaganism."

"Samuel Simpson! I never heard you talk like that. What touched off all this reckless raving?"

"Aunt Drucilla did! Drucilla Burby! That amazing amazon – broad of back, narrow of mind, deep in bigotry. She says Phoebe's book is a handwriting on the

wall for Belshazzar, inferring perhaps that I am Bel. Very well, I propose to do some handwriting myself. She never did like Uncle Dex – said he had the face of a bull terrier. She was so indignant when she heard that Dexter was bound to invent a chain of tempermental restaurants. She is dead set against the idea of a church dinner; says it makes the House of God savor more of soup than of sanctimony. But my book shall refute her with great appetizing gusto."

"Very well, Sam, exalt your good cookery creed to a new cult and call it the Church of the Loaves and Fishes. Now that you have expressed your flare-back to Drucilla's letter are you through with that subject?"

Sam went to pour more punch, and while he quaffed I said, *"When your prairie fire of self-exaltation has burned out I have something to say. I have here a letter...."*

Sam put down his glass and interjected, *"Oh that letter! That gad-fly letter! It has been stabbing at me all this maddening evening! Judge Byng! My Dumptiad shall delineate him mighty well. That jolly duffer, that buffoon and bluffer – quack in law – quack in business, quack in politics – professional in poker. Burly belly – bushy beard – barn door ears – and a strawberry nose which never got its tint from berries. He sticks pins in the lapel of his coat – strikes matches on his trousers – and always says Topeekie for Topeka."*

Nonchalantly I waved the letter as a signal to be attentive.

"Here! Gimme that letter. I can read the thing faster than you."

Sam grabbed the letter from my grasp. I clutched his arm, but with a savage thrust of his elbow he sent me reeling backwards until I almost lost my balance. I charged upon him. Once more he fended me away.

"But Sam! That's a private letter – all to me – and there are some personal remarks never intended for you."

"All the more reason I should read it. Stand off, you furious mouse! Sit down I say! This letter concerns me, therefore I will read the damned thing."

My hopes crumpled before the headstrong will of Samuel Simpson. I dropped to the divan and all I could say was, *"This is positively his last letter."*

"Dear boy Bernie! I have been cursed with final letters all this evening. The gods be thanked if this is the final sting. Byng's letters have been after me like horse flies all summer. I answered none. So now he takes to writing you. What does he say?"

Sam swallowed the remainder of his punch, cleared his throat and prepared for the ordeal of reading.

The first sentence to catch Sam's eye was this one:

> ***I own the patent on a new kind of brick that can outlast the fires of hell.***

"Oh, Bernie! He wrote that same quirk about hell in a letter to me last month. He can pave all hell with his bricks so far as I care."

Silently Samuel perused the letter; then he repeated aloud:

> ***You boys must not forget that these two jobs will be reserved for you no later than Monday next. No later. Report for work then or never.***

"We should decide tonight, Sam."

"Well, Bernie, this is only Thursday night. Let us put off Monday's botheration until after your birthday. Let us devote tomorrow night to this paving of hell."

Nervously I said, *"Agreeable to me, Sam. We will read it tomorrow night. Now please hand back my letter."*

"Not so soon! There is something you don't want me to read. Where is that something?.... Ah, maybe this is the one."

Then he read:

> ***Sam is too much of a dreamster. In due time he will discover that his garden of dreams yields a harvest of nightmares. He better hitch that brilliant mind of his to a wagon instead of a star if he hopes to reap a crop of spondulix before he dies. Drooling in day-dreams brings home no bacon.***

"There's Byng's hog-wagon philosophy well worded for you. He wants to change me from a dreamster to a teamster. Profitable brilliancy! It tickles me to read this stuff. Let's see what more he says.... Ah, here's a dreamy gem! Hear this!"

He read:

> ***Not long ago I mailed a dandy dream to Sam. It was a blueprint of our new machine for pressing brick clay. A blueprint is the right kind of a dream for a promising young man. It leads to a profitable output of actual goods.***

"Bernie, this letter is a nightmare to me. Now listen to this one:"

> ***Sam is loaded with dynamic energy that will smash to the front as soon as he puts on the gear of a go-getter in the world of business. I love the boy. I promised his father I would find him a job. Here is the job.***

With a knowing look at me, Sam remarked, *"Byng loves me! When he was a police judge in this town he pompously declared that I was the ring leader of the rowdy riot of students who were celebrating our victory in that great football game. He threatened to fine me for contempt of court for what I said. So Byng loves me now! Well let me read some more of these classic quirks and quips."*

He skimmed the letter further then he exclaimed, *"Here's a monumental quibble. This one makes me mad."*

A moment of silent reading then Sam read aloud:

> ***Today Samuel Simpson stands at the cross-roads of his life. It is yes or no to this way or to that one: to the path of perspiration which leads to eventual retirement on a respectable income, or to the path of a playboy which leads to the poor house. Time is money, Sam has spend-thrifted too many of his days dilly-dallying in cow pastures and writing down the buzzing of the bees and the warbling of the orioles all in a monumental jugglery of high falutin words.***

Sam exploded, *"Enough of this letter – this hybrid hog-and-oriole letter – this slump from the sublime to the slime. Byng tries to appraise the song of an oriole in values of bacon. Poor Byng! He never had an ear for music. Byng! The elephant-eared. Enough of all this balderdash."*

Sam flung the epistle straight into my face. Holding my temper I pushed the letter back to his hands.

"Sam! Read the postscript of that letter while you're at it."

"Postscript! Poof! A postscript on such a letter is only a needless extra rag on the tail of an overloaded kite. I swear to read no more of that ragtailed letter."

Contemptuously he tossed the letter to the table.

My face grew hot with anger. I shouted, *"Byng is right. You can't be just a playboy all you life. You've got to do some real work in this world. Abandon all your bankrupt dreams. Don't try to mend your broken mirrors. Tune up now to a new dream of life."*

Sam turned his back to me and walked away while grumbling, *"Blue prints! Blue prints! Indigo blue prints. Waterproof dreams."*

I fairly shrieked, *"Samuel Simpson! You never dreamed of working very hard!"*

"Gentle fellow, don't rave that way about me. My past failures are nothing more than freckles on the peach of my confidence."

"I tell you here and now. Sam, I am resolved to make a new start in life beginning tomorrow morning. Next week I leave this place by myself if you refuse to go."

"A new start! An old idea of yours! You are an old chap in many ways. Let me see – how old will you be tomorrow? Twenty-three or twenty-four?"

"As though you did not know! And you only a year older than I. Now don't get sardonic."

"Well, I want no more hog-wagon talk tonight. I shall make no new start tomorrow. I'll keep on climbing Mount Helicon and you can bet your life I'll not come down to worship Byng's blue prints of the Golden Calf."

"Turn your back on the Calf and you face the Wolf."

"Then what? The Wolf. He hushes every song I sing; he frightens every hope." The bawling of the Calf kills all my song."

"Had you read that postscript you would hear the pit-a-pat of the Wolf right behind you now."

"And what matters Wolf or Calf to me of the Lions? I will never turn from my stars. Mount Helicon. I will not drop my baggage now at the half-way-up and turn back. No. I will climb Mount Helicon if it takes all my life to climb! May God restore that PRELUDE I lost awhile ago."

I folded up the rejected letter. "Have your way, Sam. Leave the end of Byng's letter until tomorrow after my birthday feast is over."

Sam strode to the big globe in the library, planted his finger in the center of America, on the state of Kansas and then he set the globe spinning on its axis.

"I want to do something that nobody else has done. I want to set all Kansas singing a joyous cicada song. So tomorrow afternoon you must go with me to the country to collect a lot of live cicadas for the cages in my cricket room downstairs. I am sure they will sing there and that I shall be able to translate their songs."

This unexpected proposition disappointed me. I rose up in reaction. *"Why Sam! We are to go to Kanopolis tomorrow afternoon and take an evening birthday lunch in the Saucisserie. You agreed to go. Don't you remember? You don't? ... but you promised to show me what the Saucisserie and its kitchen are like, and to introduce me to the clever cook who invented that famous super-sausage Sam."*

I had, at least , arrested his attention. He stared at me. One of his eyebrows went up while the other went down, and that was always a sure indication of rumination on the part of Samuel. I still had hopes.

In commiserating tone of voice, he said, *"You are so devoid of delicate discrimination. Clever cook! Why Bernie! Aristide is a French savant, an artist, and a poet who has taken to elegant cookery just for a pastime. Super sausage! What a defamatory way you have of describing excellent earthly things. Super-sausage! I suppose his famous onion soup means only pot-likker to you. Artistide writes the most imaginative menus, illustrates them with marginal drawings of his own. Super-sausage! Aristide keeps the compound of that viand all a secret. He makes every one to order, grinds the meat himself, then he fires them and blends the gravy with lager beer; next he rubs a warm platter with garlic to make a foundation; then come trimmings of tripe and truffles and pixy puff mushrooms. Finally the whole creation is coddled to a finish in an oven; and forth comes a triumph of gastronomy, an aromatic viand in state, with the elegant brown of a Stradivarius. Super-sausage! Wait 'til you see its proper name on the menu."*

"You rouse in me great expectations. It will be a unique finish for my birthday. And why not have Byng with us? You know he tells such funny stories after beer."

Quizzically Sam looked at me. Did he surmise some trick, some trap, some stratagem when I mentioned Byng and beer?

"Have I said I would go?"

"Well, you never said you would not go." I answered somewhat nervously.

"Very well. We will toss a coin to decide right now as to Byng and beer."

Sam went directly to an oriental teak-wood chest of drawers from which he plucked a twenty-five cent piece.

"Chance or choice. Which shall it be, Bernie?"

"Have your own way, as usual, Sam."

"All right. I'll say heads for hunting cicadas, and you say tails for the shrine of the sacred sausage. Eh?"

There was a tricky twinkle in his eye. He snapped the coin high up above his head and let it fall behind his back. I saw it face-up on the carpet. My quick foot stamped upon the coin. Standing thus I said, *"Chance is a lazy man's god – the fond hope of a fool. Sam Simpson! Where is your judgement? And you at the crossroads tonight."*

I had circumvented chance by force of will. What next? The tricky smile expanded to a grin on the face of Samuel.

"Serve mammon and win the world. An ancient and a modern temptation!"

Walking away in a stage strut he retorted, *"Keep your heavy foot on the symbol of Caesar. It fell face-up. I abide by the face on the coin under your foot."*

"How do you know it fell heads up?"

His grin gave way to laughter. He rested his hands on my shoulder and replied, *"That quarter has a face on either side. Two coins were halved and fused together."*

"Why Sam! That is deliberate cheating! It is worse than straight-out gambling! How dare you?"

"How dare you stamp your foot upon what you guessed to be an honest fling."

"Who cut that coin?"

"Some clever swindler. Uncle Dex obtained it for his collection of gambler's devices. This whole cabinet is stuffed with dice of ancient days and modern," said Sam while he replaced the two-faced coin.

"Now don't gamble away your future, Sam. Take a quick inventory of your past life. Have you ever made a home run on your dreams?"

"Well, who has?"

"You have never cashed in on your writings. Publishers reject you. Phoebe rejects you. And now Hecktor Byng bobs up with a sure thing! I promised your father on the day before he left us that I would persuade you to consider the first good business job that came your way. Remember your father. At least consider this job in deference to his wishes. Yonder hangs his picture looking directly at you."

I believe Sam saw the tear in my eye as I said this.

He looked upon the portrait and also upon the miniature picture of his mother. For a moment in silence he stood with a fatuous stare in his eyes. Then he quaffed the last of the punch, and resuming a stage strut he said, in histrionic soliloquy, *"Forks of the road! Which fork for Sam Simpson? The long, long thorn-bordered path which is paved with stardust or the short, broad busy way paved with vitrified brick? I say, my fair play pal, this million dollar decision is not one for a whirling coin, and it is not one for a timid chap of the House of Virgo. No. I shall call the numbers of the Chaldeans to decide that question."*

Once more Samuel went to the cabinet of gamester's playthings and gathered a handful of ancient Chaldean dice. He came forward with them displayed in his hand and repeating this exhortation which Uncle Dex was fond of repeating in a throw of dice:

> **"What ho! Bring dice and good wine!**
> **Who cares for the morrow?**
> **Live! So calls grinning Death,**
> **Live! For I come to you soon!"**

"Look, Bernie, on each of these dice is a little character curved in at both ends somewhat like a pretzel. Well that is the Chaldean emblem of the celestial Lion. Now, to decide tomorrow's afternoon, we will race the Lion against the sausage. I'll stand by the Lion. The afternoon of your birthday! Shall it be spent in sweet pastures singing with cicadas, or in Kanopolis with a stately sausage? O Stars of Virgo, now potent in the heavens, bear witness to this race between the porkers and the Lion. What ho! Stars of the Lion, the Swine of the Earth challenge you to a race! Here goes!"

The hurly-burly dice then tumbled on the green felt of the billiard table. Helplessly I looked on and listened while the fate of my birthday was being told in these hectic incoherent proclamations, *"First cast. The Porkers wildly dash to the fore. A pig always makes a good show at the start of a race."*

"Cast two. Oh Astral Virgo, behold that cast. The Porkers still pound on ahead."

"Now let the Chaldean numbers speak for the third time. What see we now? The Porkers get their second wind and kick dust in the eyes of the lion."

"Now for another cast. What says this? Neck-and-neck."

"Cast again. And ho what? The stars in their courses smile on the Lion. The Porkers are winded and drop to the rear. Now for the final fateful cast. Hold your breath till they fall. They're off! See them race across the cloth. Now count them up. There you have it. The swine, the whole herd of them runs to a suicide in the sea. They lost the race."

"A lion-roaring birthday is decreed for the child of Virgo. I shall hitch my chariot to a team of lions!"

"Hitch to a comet!" I snapped as I rose up to leave the room *"The sooner you come to a grand smash the sooner you wake up to sense."*

"Restrain yourself now, you gentle child of Virgo. Sit down! The Dice of Fate have ruled out sausage for tomorrow. Besides, these are the days of Canis Major, dog days, when sausage is quite out of season. Sit down I say! And calm your filibuster mind for the rest of the night. I have been so bedeviled with letters all this day and evening and so heckled by your hacking voice that I was never as close to being crazy as now. I say, for the rest of the night let the Lion and Lamb lie down in peace."

"Anything you say, Sam."

"Then throttle all the steam whistles of your mechanical brain. Stop the whirling of your mental merry-go-round. Stop the Lion and the Wolf and the Calf and the Astral Ass. Give me nothing but soothing voices just now."

Sam flung open the door that led to the basement room. A chorus of crickets greeted our ears.

"Hear that choir of midgets of the night? They assure me – they assuage me – they cast out devils from my mind."

He began pacing the carpet and muttering to himself while rubbing his palms. So I suggested, *"I say, Sam, while your crickets are soothing the night, suppose we have a night story."*

Samuel and I frequently spent the last evening hour in reading to each other.

"Go ahead Bernard! A night story! I need the sleep of a mummy tonight. Gives us a story Then give us sleep."

"Prose or poetry, Sam?"

With eyes on the ceiling, he replied, *"Oh some lovely fiction on the borderland of poetry and prose. Some anodyne to ease the ache of actualities. and while I listen to your reading that lost prelude may come back to me."*

I strolled before the books that lined the wall, calling titles as I passed. Here were old books, new books, all kinds of books – a bewilderment of books – testifying what insatiable and omnivorous bibliophyles Samuel's people had been. Some of these books were older than the advent of printing and some were even older than the English language. Here were ancient books lettered in Greek or Latin. Among them was a Greek Gospel lettered on parchment pages which had aged into pleasing hues of purple, and there was a superb medieval volume in Latin with colored uncials illumined with pure gold and exquisitely lettered on vellum made from the skins of unborn lambs. There was a Banquet of Tremalchio by Petronius hand-lettered in Latin. Some of these examples had at one time belonged to potentates of Venice, and some were examples from old monasteries. None of the old books would do for a reading tonight so I passed to the shelves of modern volumes but to every title I suggested Samuel promptly answered, *"No."*

"I am at the end of the shelves, Sam."

"Go on to the French section."

I passed by all the recent French editions and came to the cabinet of delicious old books which had won the affections of Uncle Dexter. He had picked them up in antiquarian shops in Europe and in book stalls along the Seine in Paris. Among these exotics were sumptuous editions dealing with perfumes, or jewels or rare wines, and some of them were epicurean dissertations on the art of dining. I was more fluent in French than Samuel, although during all his life a French governess had been in the home.

"Well, Sam, here I am at the case of the old French books that Uncle Dexter loved so dearly."

"Go no farther. Pluck out some ambrosial tale told in honied words, a tale of tipsifying fancies told just for the joy of telling – something with no preaching and no teaching – a story that transforms realities into fancies and disappointments into dreams. Oh something that's simply a beautiful tale."

My eye fell on the big fat volume on the bottom shelf. It bore the title *Les Contes Du Turk.*

"Here, Sam, is the very book, The Tales of the Turk.

"There you have it! Be that our reading! That amber-toned book is the very tale after a night like this."

It was a massive volume, an old French rendering of some disconnected tales akin to the Abrabian Nights and illustrated with hand-colored gravures of the eighteenth century. I always read from this book in English and whenever I found the text obscure or obscene I made free translations of my own. Samuel little dreamed how much of myself he heard when I read him a *Tale of the Turk: The Dream Weaver.*

From the cabinet I lifted *ce vieux bouquin* whose pages were yellow and aromatic with age. The pigskin covers were heavy with big bosses of green jade encased in old silver filigree, and robust latchets of carved silver clasped these covers shut. I installed the volume on an antique reading rack. I unlocked the beetle-bitten binding and flung open the pages. Forth came an odor like that which sleeps in old oriental embroideries. The pages were much worn along the edges and some were loose from the binding.

Samuel cushioned himself on the divan and said in a snoozing voice, *"Now if I fall asleep please punch me awake. So give us one more bed-time story from that intoxicating opiate book."*

The pages fell open at the *Tale of the Moon Girl,* a tale which neither of us had read. Like all the others, this one was a saraband of sensuous fancies and vague allegories told in the imaginative anarchy of oriental story tellers.

When I called out the title Samuel responded, *"Homage to the Moon Girl! Your eyes have been blind to her; now let us hear of her. If God had forgotten to make the moon where would our finest fancies be today? Where our rarest romance – our poetry music and art? On with your reading."*

Never until now had I read to Samuel any story which so possessed him – which so metamorphosed him. To Sam it was the allegory of his life. It became his monitor – his fixed idea. It made him more of an egocentric – of a fatalist – and of a believer in his stars. This tale was the last straw on the back of his intellectual equilibrium which already bore the burden of the letter from Phoebe plus the letter from Drucilla plus the letter from Byng.

Therefore, to explain the extraordinary career of Samuel Simpson subsequent to this ominous night of moonlight perfumed with petunia, tuberose and Havana, I must needs digress from the narrative to render a translation of the *Tale of the Moon Girl,* omitting, for brevity's sake, many of its elaborate and detailed descriptions.

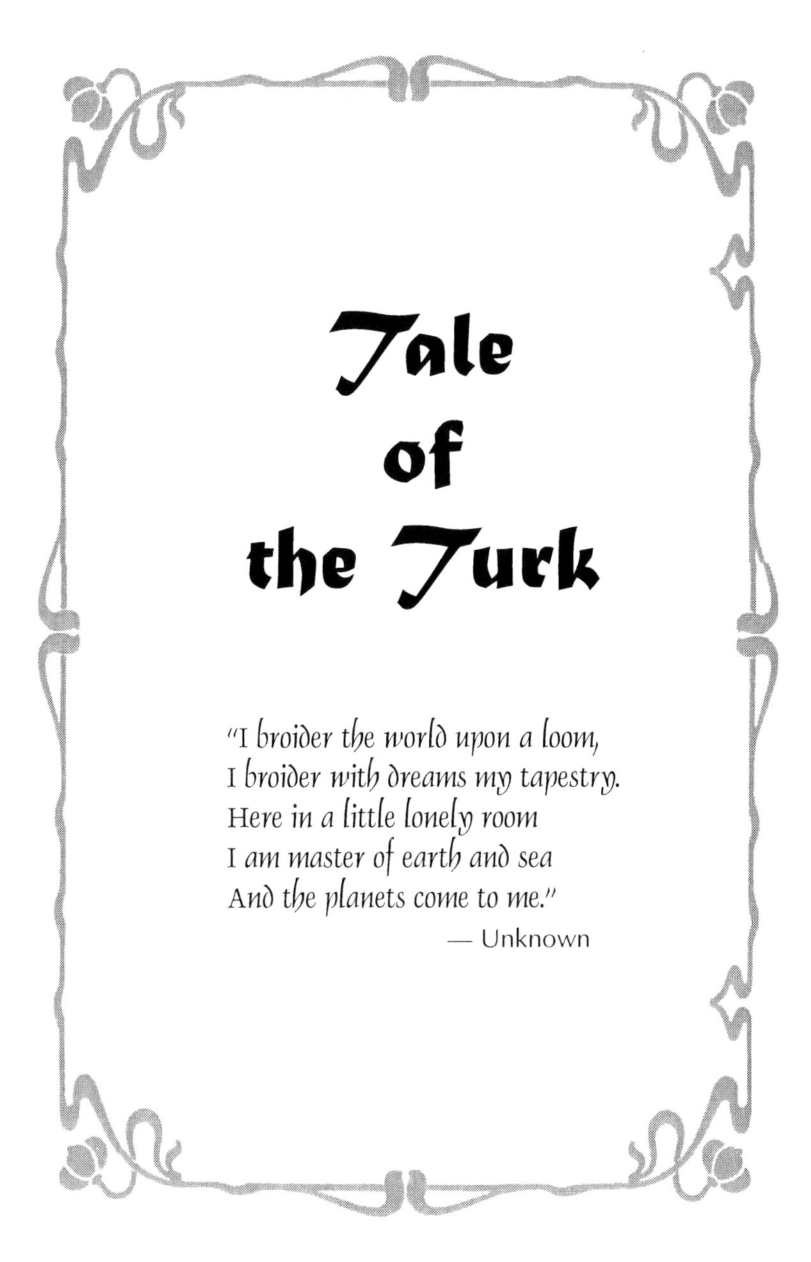

Tale of the Turk

"I broider the world upon a loom,
I broider with dreams my tapestry.
Here in a little lonely room
I am master of earth and sea
And the planets come to me."

— Unknown

"And the only world is the world of my dreams
And my weaving the only happiness
For the world is only what it seems,
And who knows but that God, beyond our guess,
Sits weaving a world out of loneliness."

— Arthur Symons
The Loom of Dreams

"O sickle of moonlight declining
Reflected by desolate waters,
O sickle of silver, what dream-fashioned harvest
Is stirred by your gentle resplendence below."

— D'Annuncio

"Her eyes the glow-worm lend thee,
The shooting stars attend thee;
And the elves also,
Whose little eyes glow,
Like sparks of fire, befriend thee."

— Robert Herrick
Night Piece to Julia

Chapter One

The Dream Weaver

n days of yore there dwelled in the city of Ingdad a weaver and a soothsayer in a comradeship that was enduring and endearing. The weaver was of kindly mein, and all day long he sat in the seclusion of his modest estate threading into his fabrics the patterns and symbols which he visioned in dreams. At night he studied the stars.

The weaver had an only child, Ali, a lad of comely feature and symmetrical stature, and of a demeanor and deportment as might beseem a youth of noble breeding. All day he applied his fingers to the craft of weaving. At night he studied music and the works of the poets for he had a gift of making lyrics of his own.

The soothsayer was wise in auguries, alchemies and astrologies. He knew which stars were lucky and which were baleful. He knew to cast a horoscope, to foretell a future, to extract a perfume, and to prescribe which amulets a man should wear and on which days. To his mansion came all manner of men. The wise and the regal brought gifts of noble perfumes and exotic unguents sealed in magic gourds and in jeweled caskets of silver and gold.

The soothsayer had an only child, Leonorina, a damsel of exalted beauty, quick-witted and prudent, lithesome as a branchlet of the willow, and with a waist so slender-fine that people often called her the "Sickle of the Moon." She was wise in her father's wizardries and cunning in the witcheries of love which had been confided to her by her departed mother, and she loved the fair sayings of the poets.

Ali, the son of the weaver, was desperately enamored of the daughter of the seer, but to none in Ingdad he told his secret. In the mansion of the seer this lad was wont to display his weavings, and there he would sing his lyrics to Leonorina while he fixed upon her his large eyes dark and deep as desert wells. But the coy damsel was indifferent to his tapestries and she greeted his eloquence with waggishness and wit.

Now this town of Ingdad was no mean place. It reposed in a lush oasis known as the Eye of the Desert, well set with tall palm trees and shrubbed with rose and jasmine and divers sweet smelling growths. The town was snuggled close to the base of a precipitous mountain wall from which opened a mysterious tunnel called The Mouth of Hell because of its rumblings and sulphurous vapors. This tunnel-mouth yawned directly into the central avenue of Ingdad which, straight and wide and lined with tall date palms and set with shrines and temples of the Gods, crossed the city from the Hell Gate to the Gate of Heaven and thence straight across the level desert to the distant marts and minions of the world. The city had shrines and temples to divers gods and the most beautiful of them was the Shrine of the Moon. To Ingdad came many a caravan to barter for its silks and spiceries and attars brewed from magic plants and for potent amulets and also for its fabrics wonder-woven and dream-pictured.

When the weaver was about to die he said, *"Beloved son, I go now to meet thy mother in the realms beyond. Treasure in thy memory these my parting words:*

"Thou art poor in purse but star-endowed. Our worthy friend, the soothsayer, hath cast thy horoscope which I have kept secret until now fearing that as a youth thou wouldst misuse or squander a potent astral wealth which is thine. Thy birth was in the season when the Sun was a guest in the House of the Lion, and in the hour between the dawn and the sunrise, when the Morning Stars were Jupiter and Venus, and when the crescent of the Moon was bright between the Lord Star and the Love Star. In that portentous moment a shooting star streamed athwart this celestial assemblage and, like Lucifer, fell to earth where it awoke a wind known as the Wind of the Streaming Star, and known also as the Wind of the Gabalouk. This is thy tutelary star and this is thy Wind Genius.

"Exhort the Lion of the Stars for courage, and the Lord Star, Jupiter, for wisdom. For the Song of Songs supplicate the Love Star Venus, the star of the silver horns, Astarte. But be ever mindful of thy Streaming Star who roameth at will through all the Houses of Heaven, and who roameth the earth as a wind. He is the Jester of the Stars and he findeth out their secrets. He knoweth even how the Lion vainly seeks the love of the evanescent ever-changing Sickle of the Moon.

"Much have I fathomed of realities in Dreamland and of shoddings and shams of this world. The only worthful thing on earth is wisdom. Now there is a certain fountain that singeth words of wisdom at the end of the world. Therefore, seek the Well at the World's End.

"All things in this world are made of dreams. Real things are only in the realm of Dreamland where reigns an eternal moonlight which doth cast upon this world

shadows of the immortal shapes that abide up there. Everything in this world is fashioned on a dream – everything we see, hear, taste or touch – everything we think or know – all these are but the shadows of Ideals moon-cast out of Dreamland. Up there abide the eternal Ideals or patterns of all shapely things – patterns of the snowflakes that last here but a moment, patterns of the traceries we find on the velvet wings of moths who flit through their fleeting hour or two of life in darksome nights and die at dawn. Here are patterns of the day blossoms and of the pallid blooms of night, and the patterns of the fluting of a seashell and of the crystalline forms in adamantine stones. Every thing around us is a fragment of a noble dream. Therefore, seek the dream which each thing represents. Therefore, seek in Dreamland for the patterns of thy weavings.

"In Dreamland are even the Ideals of the winds – the patterns of the sportive little whirlwinds and of the sea lifting typhoons – of the soft winds that whisper of love and the terrible tornados – aye the winds of good fortune and the ill winds that never blow good. Therefore, learn the language of the winds, for life flows as the wind blows, we know not why nor whence nor whither. We are at the whims of the winds. Each man is wind-wafted to his destined end as is the heaven-dropt snowflake. We spend our earthly days wind-guided through a shadow show whose meaning only the Master of Ideals knows. To know the meaning of life's Shadow Show, seek in Dreamland for the Shadow Casters.

"I told thee thy Wind Genius hath the name of the Gabalouk. Now I inform thee of the evocative wish-word which will summon and compel him to thine aid. That word is **Bélhamarámara**. *But never repeat this word unless in dire distress."*

"Lay up for thyself a treasury of dreams. Every man's

life is but his dream of life. The birth of a new dream is as the rising of the Morning Star; the death of a cherished dream is cruel as the grave. Tune thy dream of life to the universe, for the universe is the Dream of God."

"There is in Dreamland a being of supernal beauty whose shadow on the earth hath the magic of a moonlight which converts a stony desert land to beauty. Her shadow maketh stones to see and stones to sing, and it awakeneth a fountain of living water in a rainless land. The poets know her has the MOON GIRL because she wakes their minds to moonlight. But that is not her name in Dreamland. She hath a thousand names on earth but only one in Paradise.

Blest among men is he on whom the MOON GIRL smiles, for straightway her smile restoreth to the quick that which had long been dead within him, and he is reborn to new courage and new yearnings. She cometh down to earth at times to sojourn in divers places. Seek thou the MOON GIRL and find out what her name is. She alone can tell the secrets of the Heavenly Spheres."

When the soothsayer was about to die he said to Leonorina, *"Beloved daughter, cherish these my final counsels: I devise to thee an estate abundant in precious stones and perfumes and sibylline volumes of forgotten lore. But there is a certain jewel that I have not, and also a perfume and a precept of the sages.* ***This jewel is known as the Philosopher's Stone; the perfume is that of the Celestial Lily and the Precept of the Sages is the Saying that Sings.***

"As to perfumes, I devise to thee a symphony for thy nostrils. In this palace are coffers filled with essences from the world's four quarters - musk and myrrh and frankincense from the Far East – spikenard and marjoram from Mesopotamia – sandalwood and cedar from Persia – and ambergris from the great Sea Ocean. But

among these odors one is lacking. It is the odor that was cherished by the high-born maids and matrons of old Egypt, the odor of the Celestial Lily, and known in Palestine as Perfume of Great Price.

"I leave thee vitric gems that glow with internal fires and which inform the owner of approaching friend or foe. Thou hast aquamarines and moonstones in all magic hues. Thou hast bright gems from the mountains and the mines and mysterious jewels from caves deep in the vast Sea Ocean. But in this hoard of treasure one gem is lacking – the Philosopher's Stone.

"I have initiated thee in divers wizardries, and thy mother hath instructed thee in sundry witcheries. Thy tutors have schooled thee in the precepts of the sages. But there remaineth yet one saying which I have not recovered from wizard, witch, or wise man, or from old scrolls of ancient wisdom. It is the Saying that Sings. It hath the perfume of the blossoms of the Tree of Knowledge. It is the soul of every song. Beyond the truth of that saying man need not go. Short of this saying no one can be wise."

"Therefore, my Leonorina, my sole heritor, when suitors seek thy hand, and forsooth many a suitor shall come, be coy with them all, but give thy heart and hand to him only who knoweth the Saying that Sings, and who beareth that Egyptian perfume and who weareth the Philosopher's Stone."

After the weaver died the son assumed the title of Ali the Weaver. He set up his loom in his garden hedged and shrubbed with jasmine, rose, amaranth and black-rooted moly. This garden of incense was kept green all the year by a little spring that gurgled up from the stony sands. Here the happy grasshoppers chirped all day; in the dusky hours the fire flies danced to silent rhythms; and in the sable hours was the sound of zooming beetles.

But never a dream came to Ali by night or by day, and he began to despair of finding that wonderful Dreamland of which his father had told him. Therefore he contented himself with weaving into his work such patterns as had been left to him by his father who had copied them out of Dreamland.

After her father's death Leonorina took on a life of festive fashion. She equipped the enlarged palace with liveried servants, Abyssinian slave girls, Nubian eunuchs, music girls and diaphanous dancers. On her estate she installed a chapel of Isis. She entertained people of talent and of high degree. Gay companions, who gathered on her lawn on festival occasions were regaled by the music maids and by the mystic maids who repeated obscure litanies of forgotten cults and by the recitations of the poets and by the tellers of tales so enthralling that they kept the star-eyed guests wide-eyed and awake during late hours in the moonlight.

Through the aid of witchcraft Leonorina invented a golden lamp stand with the form of a seven-branched tree. From each branch depended seven lamps filled with aromatic oils of sundry powers and each lamp had a flame-color and an incense of its own. By blending certain of these flames Leonorina could give to any face whatever aspect might disport her caprice. She could make a face beautiful or noble or clownish, and this aspect would endure for a phase of the moon. She could make a cat look like a rabbit or a leopard like a goat. She gave to Ali the expression of a clown. This made the people laugh outright in his face, and even the muleteers in the narrow lanes pushed him aside for their pack-asses.

But Ali continued to nurse the gorgeous pains of his unrequited love for his heartless sorceress.

Now Ali had a foster brother, Ferista by name, who was his faithful and devoted Fag. One day the Fag said,

"Make an end of weaving carpets which nobody cares to buy. There is naught of inspiration in this town. Thy features grow more clownish every day and thy purse grows thinner all the while. Have done with dreams. There is naught of value in this lodge with its old worm-bored furnishings and that old stone lamp overhead. Sell all that thou hast and be off to the weal and wealth of the world."

"By the light of that lamp of beryl, my father made many a noble weaving."

"But he left no riches when he died. Come, let us cast our lot with the next caravan. Be off to the world, O Ali, and win for thyself wealth and fame and a wife beautiful and richly dowered."

But what would man be without Utopia?
He must always aim at the unattainable in order to
realize the attainable and to make at least one
step forward.

— Unknown

"We are such stuff as dreams are made on
and our little life is rounded with a sleep."

— William Shakespeare

Chapter Two

Ali Encounters The Turk

Came the day when into Ingdad rode an itinerant merchant on a milk-white camel caparisoned with little golden balls, and attended by four Nubian swordsmen on black donkeys. He took his accustomed place amiddle-most of the Market Square. At sight of him the crowd acclaimed: *"The Turk! The Turk!"*

From mouth to mouth the tidings spread that Zoumi Aazou, the Turk was come – Zoumi, the teller of tales, He was also known as the Merchant of Dreams because all of his wares seemed somewhat bound up with a dream. He sold Dream Books and birth stones and amulets and talismans; he told fortunes, cast horoscopes, blended love powders and eye powders and dainty pollen powders which restored to wan cheeks the Bloom of the Dawn. He sold candied fruits from Persia and cordials brewed in Kashmir and corked in phials made in Cathay. He had engaging perfumes of sundry sort and jewelry fraught with enchantments.

Zoumi Aazou spread out his goods in the Square and while waiting for people to buy he beguiled them with tales the likes whereof had never been heard. People forsook their occupations and forgot their meals to listen to these Tales of the Turk as he sat crosslegged on a rug which bore a square cross in the middle. On his head was a crimson turban adorned with a jeweled crescent. His face was florid, his eyes were blue, his beard was white and bushy. His mantle was a dye of bluish green broidered with purple and gold, and his jeweled slippers turned up at the tips.

He interpreted dreams, and to those who were not dreamers he recounted such tales as made them ever afterwards seem living in a dream. The Turk challenged all to question him. If correctly he made answer then the questioner must buy from him; if not, then Zoumi gave a premium. To him came people of high degree and low – came foplings and bumpkins and fawn-eyed damsels reared in sumptuous houses – came consequential matrons neck-bound with heavy strands of beads and ankle-bound with bands of gold bossed with jades – came also wastrels and gamesters and idle sons of patrician families.

Zoumi had a ready tale for each and all. He enthralled the romantic fawn-eyed damsels with the Island of the Moon, the isle of love and rapture, where the jeweled sands sing in the margin between the high tide and the low and croon when one treads upon them or smites them with a stick. These sands hold priceless pearls large as tear-drops and also precious stones that glow with internal fires and to be gathered only in a darksome night.

A voyage to this isle is beset with many perils. The shores are infested with cocodrills, the great sea-reptiles, which leap even to the deck of a vessel to devour the men; and there are mighty tides there that foam over reefs of obsidian sharp as sword blades.

Many a ship hath never returned from its quest of the isle, and many a captain hath returned grey-haired from a fruitless voyage. But a passage to these warm, soft singing sands is easy enough if the mariner knoweth to trim his sails and chart his course by the Moon and the Wandering Stars. But happy the man or maid who gaineth these delectable shores. There the dwellers enjoy a lasting youthfulness. They disport themselves in games and songs of glee-men and in dramas and dainty foods. In dreamy afternoons they drowse in the zone of shade where the forest meets the beach or they saunter through the sable groves which shelter little oracles of the Sibyls who tell fortunes or whisper of the mysteries of love and how it may be gained or lost. But Zoumi refused to chart the damsels thitherward because that could be granted only to a man.

To the men of noble families Zoumi related of the Genii of the Winds and how they guide the destinies of men. He told of the Winds of Fortune and the Ill Winds of Misfortune – told them of the Wind of Chance which favors or disfavors all the gamesters – told them of the Wind of Wisdom which bloweth high above all other Winds. Then he told them of the fabulous Aeolian Cavern of the Winds which is in the heart of the Mountains of the Moon which stand forever ice-capped in Africa's hottest zone and where gather all the Wind Genii of the World. In this cave may be garnered the lucky stones of earth, and gems for crowns for tiaras and for diadems and for scepters and handles of swords. Happy the man who hath the potent talisman to admit him to this cave , but if he hap to be in disfavor of the Winds promptly a tempest spews him forth to certain death.

When the youths would ask Zoumi to tell what incantation could exorcise the Wind of Chance, he would snap his finger in their faces and exclaim, *"Thy words*

Zoumi Aazou

disclose thyself to be a fool. A wise man would have asked for the influence of the Genius of the Overwind, because that Genius knoweth the wiles and ways of all the other winds."

In the afternoon of an appointed day came Leonorina and her retinue of maids to question Zoumi Aazou and to inspect his goods. At sight of her Zoumi rose upright and exclaimed, *"Back with you all! Back and away! For cometh now the adorable daughter of the soothsayer, and her desires and questions are not for vulgar ears."*

At this command the crowd withdrew to long distance or they quit the Market for the day. There remained near Zoumi only an aged hump-backed woman seated on the ground beside her humble store of kitchen ware made of the shell of gourds. Ali betook himself to a place far removed from hearing, but he watched Leonorina with the eyes of an eagle.

Zoumi saluted and salaamed. *"Worthy princess, daughter of the renowned soothsayer, I bow to thy distinguished presence. I have visited thy father in his day and have transferred to him many an example of superlative virtue. Honor my store of gadgets and trinkets with thy discerning eye, and whether aught or naught shall find favor in thy fancy, I shall count thy coming as an honor."*

Quickly the Turk spread forth the multitudinous members of his store.

"Wise Turk, I seek what is not to be sensed by nostril, tongue or eye. I seek some words of wisdom."

"A worthy wish, forsooth. I await thy question most exalted damsel."

"Repeat to me the Saying that Sings."

With troubled face the Turk replied, *"Rather would I chart thee to the Sands that Sing – to the enchanting, jeweled, coral beaches of the Island of the Moon. I assure thee that the Song of the Sands is more enthralling to a woman than the cold words of the Wisdom that Sings."*

"Nay! Nay! Crafty Turk! Be not so evasive."

"But my fair enchantress, the Saying that Sings can be repeated only to a man, and only on the cold cap of earth's highest mountain – higher than Helicon or Olympus."

Then Zoumi hung his head and said, *"Alas that I have not granted this thy asking. Take of my goods a boon."*

Promptly he spread before her a display of bracelets and neck-bands and waist-bands and anklets and bangles of gold, and wroughten trinkets of rare invention. After he had extolled their virtues and their values Leonorina replied, *"Hast thou the Philosopher's Stone?"*

"The Philosopher's Stone! Thou art the first damsel to request that adamantine gem. Alas! That stone can be entrusted only to a man. To gain it one must journey to the end of the world. It is too rare a gem to offer to these loutish men of Ingdad. High-minded lady, I am well aware thou hast a sufficiency of gems. Perchance among my perfumes may be one to win thy favor."

Then Zoumi produced sundry pomanders and cassolettes and vinaigrettes and little jars of alabaster, jade and jasper, and each one filled with an exotic essence. Said Zoumi: *"Here is a fragrance from a flower on Mount Ida; and here is an ointment and an unguent mellowed in an ancient tomb of Egypt; here is a musk from the wings of a moth of Madagascar; here is a savor that was the choice of the Sibyl of the Oracle of Delphi; here are pollen-powders from the Honey Islets that girdle the Island of the Moon; and here is a wizard of a musk captured by night from the glands of amorous crocodiles; here is ...."*

"Hast thou the essence of the Celestial Lily?"

"Ah! That perfume! It is also known as the Odor of Isis. It hath a lure too dangerous to be spread among human-kind, and it is of such a potency that no phial or casket can contain it. It is a scent not be wasted on the snouts of Ingdad. I have it not."

"Grand Turk! When thou dost return to Ingdad redeem thy prestige by bringing me three things: the Perfume of the Celestial Lily, the Philosopher's Stone, and the Saying that Sings."

"Imperious damsel! For the quest of that stone I must adventure as did Jason for the Golden Fleece; for that Saying I must go world-wandering as did Ulysses; and to capture that Perfume of Danger I must have the courage of a Samson who tore the lion with his hands and who afterwards plucked honey from the mummied carcass of the king of beasts. Gracious Lady! Of a truth thou dost not ask for trivial favors."

Leonorina responded in wit and laughing railleries. Then she signaled her retinue to withdraw. Said she in parting, *"Zoumi! Let no word of this our parley pass to other ear."*

Promptly Zoumi gathered all his gadgets. His blackamoors rushed to his aid, and hastily they forsook the Market for the night.

There remained one solitary merchant in the square, the bent old woman who had kitchen ware for sale. Ali came forth from the place where he had stood in hiding while he looked on and wondered what questions his princess might ask of the Turk. He approached the woman.

"Good dame, what stuff and goods be thine?"

"Gourd vessels of all kinds – spoons and dippers and flasks for wine and pretty phials for perfumes."

"Of a truth they have a pleasing shape and carving."

"These were all fruited on the magic gourd vine of Jonah. Believe me, young man, he who sips and sups from a gourd of Jonah groweth in courage and wisdom."

The merchants of this market were prone to overpraise their wares, but kindly Ali answered, *"They take my eye and I am moved to purchase of them. But tell me first – why sittest thou in this hot spot displaying kitchen tools beside the gem and jewel show of Zoumi Aazou?"*

"Just to listen to the tales of the Turk."

"They say he telleth wondrous tales. They say he answereth askings. I saw a lovely damsel at question with him."

"Aye! She was a damsel of delight! She quite abashed the Turk with her lively ways and wits, and nothing of his store won of her favors."

"Oft I wonder what these lofty ladies say – and how – and wherefore. Repeat to me of her askings and I shall purchase of thy wares."

He jingled a knitted purse before her eyes.

"That I will – and gladly – for it is indeed a tale to tell."

Then with mimicry, grimace and gestures, the dame impersonated the colloquy of Leonorina and the Turk.

"Worthy dame! Thou hast so taken me with thy telling that I will purchase all thy stock and store."

Ali flung to her his knitted purse.

In the afternoon of the morrow Ali came to the Market bearing his store of weavings. It was a day of cerulean sky in which drifted many a snow-white filament of the gossamer spiders. Some of these gossamer scarfs swirled round the head of Zoumi Aazou who held his accustomed place in the square. Near the Turk sat the Gourd Woman, but her store was now of armbands, earrings, finger rings and neckbands, all fashioned with great cunning from the shells and seeds of gourds.

Side-glancing and with faltering steps, Ali encircled the group of folks gathered round Zoumi Aazou. The Turk espied him and called, *"Come hither, young man! What stuffs and goods be thine?"*

"Fabrics that beseem Emirs and Caliphs and Viceroys. Prayer rugs worthy of the Grand Sultan, and all of them beautiful with patterns from Dreamland."

The damsels tittered. The young men snickered. Old men smiled. With a saucy toss of his head, spouted off Zoumi, *"A lordly boast for a bumpkin clad in saddle cloth such as the asses wear. Peddling patterns of Dreamland! Ah, ha, ha! Think not to fob off any counterfeit on me! I am the Sultan of Dreams. I challenge thee to make good thy boast of gleaning dream-stuff. Unwrap thy carpets. I can tell."*

Proudly Ali drew himself upright and answered, *"That will I do and gladly, but first prove thyself to be Sultan of Dreams by answering what I may put to thee. I can tell."*

Again the damsels tittered and the young men made wry faces. The old men seemed astonished at this audacious challenge.

Piqued with indignation the Turk retorted, *"Saucy simpleton! Put thy question. If I prove myself the Sultan of Dreams then fling me all thy carpetries and I shall distribute them among my blackamoors. If I fail, pluck what pleaseth thee from my store ."*

This put the folks in merry mood and some of them twiddled their thumbs.

Asked Ali, *"In Dreamland, what is the name of the Moon Girl?"*

Zoumi glowered. Then he growled, *"Now who hath told thee of the Moon Girl?"*

"My father, who was sackclothed like myself, but whose soul roamed in Dreamland. Behold: I carry with me an emblem of the Moon Girl."

From within his clothing Ali withdrew a bit of silken tapestry which, on a ground of celestial blue, portrayed a mystic star above a half-seen crescent, and below this crescent was the face of a maiden miraculously portrayed in silks of rainbow dyes.

Silence gripped the Turk and all the ribald crowd. In altered tone said Zoumi, *"For that tapestry I will answer what thou asketh."*

"Not so, Grand Sultan of Dreams, I will never part with this portrait. It was retraced out of Dreamland by my father on the day after he first looked upon my mother's face. This is a dream-likeness which he beheld in the face of my mother."

In altered tone replied Zoumi, *"Ah! So thou art the son of the Weaver of Ingdad! I knew him. I have supped in his lodge. I have partaken of his porridge and his wisdom. Therefore in memory of thy father I will consider thine asking."*

"Then tell me of the Moon Girl and her celestial name."

"The Moon Girl, she hath a name too ethereal for fleshly tongues. The insect singers of the night know it well and they repeat the name in song. Learn the language of the midgets of the night."

"How may I meet the Moon Girl?"

Uplifting a finger Zoumi Aazou replied, *"She is a Mistress of Madness! Should she shed upon thee the witchery of those great eyes of hers, blue-green with lunar light, straightway all right-mindedness would flee thy skull leaving thee but a man of madness adrift in a realm of dreams, making of thee a changeling who thinketh himself to be quaffing honey of heaven while, in real truth, he is being drugged with wormwood and gall. The eyes of the Moon Girl brought ten years of war to Troy, put out Samson's eyes, and beheaded the Baptist. Her eyes can make thee blind as Samson. Her frown can thicken thy blood like tar. Wooing the Moon girl is but rolling the Stone of Sisyphus in a limbo of loneliness. If thous dost cherish peace of mind and repose of soul shut thine eyes and ears to this Mistress of Madness."*

"What is the Saying that Sings?"

"A song sung by the sands in the Desert of Loneliness."

"Where may I find these sands?"

"Ask that of the three Shrines in the Land of Stones. These Shrines are: of the Stones that Sing, of the Stones that See, and of the Stone of Silence."

"Where is the Well at the World's End?"

"Why, at the end, of course." This awoke a merriment. Zoumi added, "It is also called the Well at the End of the Way. To King David it was the Well of Bethlehem which is by the Gate. Now what other ensnaring question canst thou put to me?"

"Where may I find the finest weavings in the world?"

"Follow the drift of those gossamer spiders who fill all the sky above thy head today. Follow the spiders if thou wouldst be wise in weaving."

This brought outright laughter from the crowd. Scowling at them Zoumi barked, *"Fools laugh when unexpected truth is flaunted in their faces."*

Pointing to the wine-dark sky he continued, *"See those floating gossamer filaments. They are bearing the spiders to the Festival of Weavers which at this season takes place in the Mountains of the Moon. The world's most wondrous weavings are not done by human fingers; they are made by the clans of creeping, crawling flying midgets that dwell in the air, in the grass, in the ground and in the underground – by the multitudinous, multifarious tribes of insects."*

*"O worthy Zoumi Aazou, where may I behold the finest weaving made by human weavers, that I may look upon it and thereby learn to weave fabrics soft as moonlight and strong as thunderbolts and which will make the people say, '**Man hath not made it; only madness could have done it.**' "*

"Now thou dost bait me with a handsome question.

But thou must give me all that thou hast if I should answer that."

Ali flung him all his weavings save the image of his mother. Responded Zoumi, *"Thou hast more of property than these. In thy lodge hangeth a lamp of beryl curved like the new moon and carved on either side with the All-seeing Eye. I have seen it there. Go to! Fetch me that lamp and I will tell thee of the rarest weaving ever made by fingers."*

In brief, time Ali delivered the lamp. Then Zoumi arranged the weavings of Ali into a cushioned seat and he sat thereon. He placed the moon-curved lamp upon his knees and lighted its wick which tickled his nose with its incense.

Then he answered, *"The most wondrous weaving in the world is the seamless Robe of the Single Cloth which the Master wore on his way to the Place of the Skull. It was woven by a group of Holy Women who worked into that fabric a symbol of the Saying that Sings. It doth still retain the enduring fragrance of the Perfume of Great Price, the odor of the Celestial Lily, which was shed upon the Master at the wealthy man's banquet. Preserved with this garment is the sealed Scroll of the Dinner Dissertations in which the Master took a part. He had as good words for the well-to-do as he had for the woebegone, but his table-talks have been withheld from men thus far. This Robe and Scroll are guarded today by women in the land of Eutukia which lieth afar over the wide Sea-Ocean and which is sacred to goddess Fortuna."*

"How may I voyage to Eutukia?"

"Thou hast nothing more to give me; therefore, I have no further answer. The winds know all places in the world; therefore, go to their cave for further askings. But only a tutelary wind would respond to thee in the cave."

In exuberance cried Ali, *"I have a Wind Genius! I know his wish-word and his name. In the cave he will help me."*

"I challenge thee to speak the name."

"His name is the Gabalouk. His star is Lucifer, the Streaming Star."

Zoumi shook with laughter. Then he explained, *"The Gabalouk! The Gabalouk! Ah, ha, ha! The Gabalouk is the Wind of a Fool's Good Luck."*

Guffaws and huzzas broke from the audience, and Zoumi joined in with the laughter.

"This has been a comic show for me. Ah, ha, ha." Then pointing to the long shadows of late afternoon he added, *"I have said enough. I have heard enough. Here endeth one more day. Be off with you all!"*

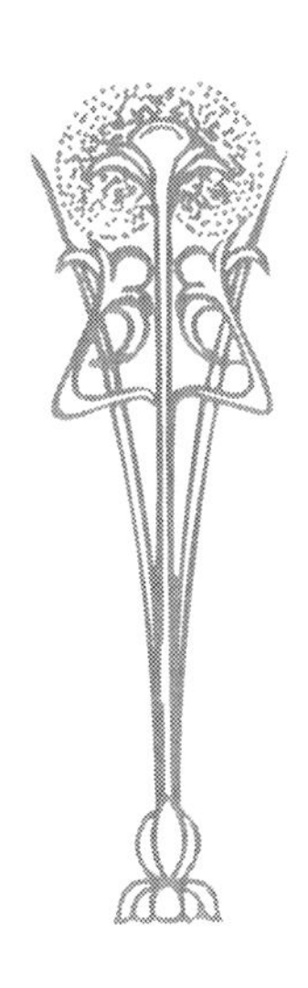

Chapter Three

Mysteries of the Moon

A single soul remained in the Market Square, the Gourd Woman standing distraught and disheveled.

"O Weaver of Ingdad! Thy tournament with the Turk hath touched me like a flame of fire! Trust not to spiders for guidance to the Cave of the Winds. I can send thee there on a camel. I heard the Turk tell of Eutukia. My sister is the queen of that country. In her land is the wonder-woven Robe embalmed in the Perfume of Great Price. To that city come men of high degree and low, and they disport themselves in divers games of chance. In that town are preserved the very dice which the soldiers cast for the Robe."

"Thy sister! And a queen! O Mistress of the Gourd Shells! Thou dost out-tell the Turk in tales. Thy sister! Little woman, methinks the tale of the Turk hath made thee mad."

"I have many sisters in this world. Some wear garbs as humble as my own; and some are bangled and

spangled with gold. Glorious among my sisters is she of the realm of Eutukia. Her name is Fortunata, and she is a devotee of the goddess Fortuna. I can direct thee to her court."

"Thy words are honey to mine ears; thine aspect is thorns to mine eyes."

"Hast heard of how Samson gathered honey from the mummy of a Lion in a land of thorns? O Weaver of Ingdad! Brave youth with unbelieving eyes! Thou hast heard from me the honey of truth."

"Wretched wight! Be thou witch or sister-queen I know not! But tell me what thy name may be."

"I am yclept Sister of the Thorns because I choose to dwell in a thorny lodge just outside the walls of Ingdad. I am also known by the pleasant name of Dame Bonnechance. But my name is Miriam – Miriam of the Crown of Thorns."

"And by what token may I know thou art of a line of queens?"

She fumbled in her purse and plucked out a ring.

"By this signet."

Ali found this ring to be of some strange metal with a most uncommon lustre and graven with an emblem of the goddess Fortuna.

Said Miriam, *"This ring might win thee entrance to the court of Sister Fortunata. It might. But she is capricious, as all men know, and it is no easy play to win and hold her favor."*

"O that she would permit me to see the Robe."

"Tell that wish to Penelope, the Mistress of Weavers in Eutukia. Show her this ring. Tell her that Miriam of the Thorns sent thee to her. She can instruct thee as to the Robe."

While Ali wavered in indecision Miriam added, *"I alone in Ingdad can send thee to the Cave of the Winds in the Mountains of the Moon. I mind to send two beasts of burden to the mouth of that cave to fetch more gourds of the Vine of Jonah. They know the way there. Load them with gourds there. They know to return of their own accord. Be thou my cameleer."*

She fitted the ring upon his finger. He made no resistance.

With his eyes on the ring he replied, *"Yesterday I gave thee all my gold. Today I gave Zoumi all my goods. What have I now of worldly stuff which might be as a boon for thee?"*

"Brave boy, I shall grant a boon to thee if be thou my cameleer. I have this day sold all my goods save this girdle. Accept it as a recompense for gleaning gourds. Thou seekest perfumes; for that reason thou wilt cherish this belt all thy days."

Her lean, long hands held forth a waist-band of uncommon contrivance, a wide belt of leather, inlaid with little phials made of gourds attached to a vine of electrum which bound them in place.

While Ali marveled at the curious carvings on the gourds the woman explained, *"In this world are seven super-perfumes from which all other odors are blended. The inscription on each phial reads thus:*

Fill me with one of the divine seven and I shall
retain it until the day of judgement.

"This meaneth that the liquor in each bottle doth restore its volume whenever a drop may be dripped from it. Thou hast simply to fill an emptied phial with dew water gathered from a red rose, and that dew will change to the wine of the perfume."

"Forsooth this belt hath somewhat of a noble style."

"It is quite worthy of a satrap. It hath little secret pockets for coins or amulets or for little daggers for self defense. It is a belt of virtue."

"I will be thy cameleer."

"Come then to my thorn lodge on the morrow after tomorrow. I shall start thee on thy journey of life."

Ali returned to his lampless lodge and to Ferista, his Fag, said he, *"Now have I naught of earthly goods. I am in disfavor of all in Ingdad, even of my Leonorina. On the morrow of tomorrow let us quit this place and journey across the world."*

"Bravo, boy Ali! Bravo. Long have I yearned to escape from this desert town. Bravo! Away with our weaving of rags! Now for the ways of this world! Now for noble adventure! Wherever thou goest, Ali, there go I."

After a frugal meal the two youths retired. Ferista was soon aslumber but the ears of Ali were atingle with the voices of the myriad creatures in the tarn which separated his lodge from the lawn of Leonorina. Above the raucous voices of the bosky bog were faint echoes of instrumental music. Ali sat upright.

To himself he exclaimed, *"That music is the prelude to her birthday which falls upon tomorrow. Just now she may be on her lawn moving amidst her women like the moon among the stars."*

He surmised aright in this. But Ali knew not that Leonorina had recently become a devotee to the Shrine of the Moon nor did he know that on this night was the annual Festival of the Moon in which all the Moon Girls of the Shrine were assembled on the lawn of Leonorina to initiate her into the mysteries of the moon on this eve of her nativity. A sudden mad urge seized upon Ali. He would penetrate the tangles of the tarn just for one glimpse of Leonorina.

Ferista lay loud breathing in heavy sleep. For clothing Ali thrust his limbs into a discarded wine skin which had served as water bag in a caravan. He swathed head and hand and foot with old skins and in this ugly armor he braved the brambles, foundered through the mire, crawled under drooping branches whereon perched weird birds with fire-lit eyes and from which dangled luminous spiders. He fought his way through to the utmost edge of the tangles and there he emerged upon the clean sandy margin of a limpid pool, round as the moon, and which at this spot overflowed into the bog.

Directly in front of Ali, on the far side of the pool, was a festival of such sumptuosity that it might well have been an unexpected glimpse into Dreamland. The palace of Leonorina was in plain view. From the palace to the pool descended an alley staked with two rows of fragrant torches. Behind the torches rose dark cypress trees and half-seen in their shadows moved Nubian eunuchs with drawn scimitars. In front of the torches stood two ranks of young women facing each other in divers garb and costume. Here were girls from the Shrine of the Moon and from the Chapel of Isis and from the palace. Marching forward through these bright ranks and wrapped in a robe of white was Leonorina between two mauve-clad temple girls. Ahead of her marched a tall white-haired priestess in black leading the way to the pool. The pageant ranks saluted with uplifting arms as they passed.

Overwhelmed by all this unexpected spectacle Ali sank to the sand beneath his ugly skins and there he lay silent as a shadow.

At the water's edge the priestess proclaimed the baptism of Leonorina into the mysteries of the Moon at the hour of her nativity. Then a bevy of maidens formed a half-circle behind Leonorina and there they stood each one bare to the waist and skirted in weblike textures, some with instruments of music, and others with phials and flasks of unguents and perfumes with which to anoint their mistress on her return from the pool. Two slave girls came forth to remove the white robe. Then

Leonorina went into the pool deeper and deeper until the conscious water closed over her head. The attendants then summoned their mistress to return.

Leonorina rose like an exhalation of loveliness from the pool and proceeded to the strand where two maids enfolded her in a blanket of soft white wool. Then she stood there to be perfumed and anointed. All this took place to the vibrance of cithers softly stroked by light fingers and to the chanting of a mystic ritual of the moon.

At the close the priestess proclaimed Leonorina as one of the Sisters of the Moon. Promptly Leonorina strode to the edge of the pool, extended her arm towards where Ali lay, and in clear voice recited the mystic Exhortation to the Moon. In conclusion the black-robed priestess prophesied, *"O Leonorina of the Moon, it hath been ordained that on this thy natal day an anointed and heroic young man shall be the first to greet thee in thy palace and he will pledge himself to go in quest of the things of thy heart's desire."*

Then the whole cortege escorted white-robed Leonorina to her palace.

One by one the flames of the torches flickered out and left an afterglow of rosy embers. Silence fell upon the solitary gardens. Ali rose to his feet.

"What world is this! Have I not stumbled into the heart of Dreamland all unwitting and beheld immortal Ideals there? Have I not profaned them with uninvited eyes? Is this brown earth or is it Dreamland?"

His bare feet paced the margin of the pool until he came to where the foot of his beloved stood erstwhile. By the glow of rosy embers he beheld her very footprint in the sand and near it lay an alabaster phial of perfume carelessly dropped by one of the anointing girls. He unclasped the stopper. Forth came a fragrance to transmute body and soul. His heart dilated with a courage the likes of which he never knew; his features shaped themselves into a new harmony. Under the bewitchment of this ethereal ichor he swooned to the sand.

But not entirely aswoon lay he there. His brain was burning with the mystic Exhortation to the Moon by Leonorina. His eyes were attracted by a blue vapor which crept from the tarn and out upon the pool where, in the shape of a great disk, it lay in strange undulations. Ali felt himself more in an astral than a terrestrial world. The cool breath of the last watch of the night soothed his brow. It was the hour between the darkness and the daylight. A brace of morning stars were heralds of the sun and between these planets gleamed the slender sickle of the moon.

Ali exclaimed, *"O silent stars! My stars! Shed upon me thy sweet influence!"* Then he rose, and to the celestial sickle he repeated word after word of the Exhortation to the Moon.

Straightway awoke a commotion in the midst of the coverlet of mist and out of an upsurge flowered forth a maiden of supernal beauty. Over her figure from head to foot was a veil pale blue with Lunar light, and the meshes of this gauzy veil, were bespangled with little six-pointed stars whose light reflected in the damsel's eyes. Veiled was her face to her eyes. Above her brow burned a thin bright crescent like the moon's and above the crescent was a planet, nebulous, as though shining through tears. Thus arrayed, the Star Maid chanted, in chiming syllables, a melody which enraptured Ali's soul. All the little creatures of the bog united with her song. Her carol ended. She remained there before Ali's bewildered eyes.

"Oh song of the heart's desire! O Veiled Goddess! Who art thou?"

"I am the Voice invoked by the Exhortation to the Moon. What wouldst thou hear of me?"

The Moon Girl

"The Saying that Sings."

"My song repeated that saying in a tongue thou knowest not. The little voices of the bog are rehearsing it now."

"O thou enthralling phantasma! Thou magic of the moonlight! Lovely art thou as the new moon when she is the bright surprise between the daylight and the dark. Of a surely thou art the Moon Girl."

"Of a surely." Silently she stood with eyes star-bright and with silver sandals resting on a billow of mist above the pool.

"O celestial Moon Girl, whose veil overspreads the humblest being with a magic like a moonlight on a stony land, O Princess of Dreamland, dweller of the celestial spheres and visitor to this earth in seasons, tell me where in the orb of this earth I may find thy terrestrial dwelling place?"

"By the Well at the World's End."

"At the End of the World I shall seek thy presence. O mystic Moon Girl, when may it please thee to unveil thy face?"

"Not until the Day of the Bridegroom."

"O lady of celestial realm! What is thy name in Dreamland?"

The shrill voice of the clarion cock proclaimed the advent of daylight. Immediately the Moon Girl and the mist dissolved and garish day took over the world.

"Have all these bright visions been but figments of a dream?" cried Ali. *"Alack! I find I now cannot recall one word of the Exhortation to the Moon!"* He could not recall it on that day, nor on the next, nor thereafter.

He hastened to his lodge, and, before Ferista was awake, he donned a garb such as the pilgrims wear and he girdled his waist with the gourd belt of Miriam of the Thorns.

When Ferista awoke he cried, *"O Ali! What charm of witchcraft hath so changed thee overnight? Thy clownish face is now of noble symmetry. Thou art belted like a satrap, and meseems I sniff a regal perfume in thy makeup. How cometh all this sudden exaltation?"*

"I have seen the Moon Girl."

"Like thy father – drugged with dreams. But today we must prepare to leave Ingdad."

"Ere we depart, it concerneth me to take leave of Leonorina."

"O folly-following fellow! Only a god of fools can preserve thee! Why tempt the claws of her drowsing resentment? Hath she not scoffed thee from her presence? And told thee to thy face thou are a clown? And now – ah me – her eunuchs will cleave thee stark before her eyes! Let that drowsing tigress so remain."

"But it hath been ordained that I shall be the first to greet her in her palace and make grand announcement for the nonce. Await me here, I return anon."

Directly to the palace Ali went. A Nubian at the portals challenged,*"Who cometh here at this early hour? And by whose leave? And whence? And wherefore?"*

"As a servitor of thy princess am I come to be the first to speak a birthday pledge today. I pledge me to go as a questor through the quarters of the world to procure for her three things which she craveth but hath not."

The guardsman was much impressed by this imperious speech and by the satrapic belt and the signet ring on Ali's finger. Silently he withdrew into the antechamber. When he returned he said, *"Our princess grants thee immediate audience."*

At the approach of the Weaver Leonorina exclaimed, *"What knavery is this which I see staged before me here? Thy blood should pay for this impudent invasion of my palace by a carpet maker!"*

Ali stood before her proudly, unperturbed. As he looked upon her charm of face and perfection of figure he felt his heart beating strong against the phial of perfume which he had so lately ravished from her lawn.

"O princess Leonorina, a fortune of fate grants me to salute thee on thy birthday and to inform that on the morrow I set out in quest of things for which thy heart hath hungered," he exclaimed.

Leonorina rose speechless and with wondering eyes. Whence came this unaccustomed firmness in his voice? And that heroic aspect of his features? And why that belt of a satrap and that ring?

Then she cried out, *"Clownish fellow! What knowest thou of my fond desires? I need no advisement of a yokel as to what additional kickshaws I may fancy."*

Now she saw he was no longer of a clownish aspect, and with alarm she sensed the uncommon odor with which he was anointed. She was mystified and mortified. Two dark-skinned swordsmen then took stations on either hand of the lady.

Responded Ali, *"Princess, thou hast jewels beyond compare; thou hast perfumes beyond compare; thou hast scrolls inscribed with honied words of wisdom. But there yet remaineth for thee the Philosopher's Stone and the Perfume of the Celestial Lily and the Saying that Sings. These three treasures I shall bring to thee after many a moon."*

"And this to me! And by a weaver!" Rigid as a statue she stood a moment in deep breathings. Then a trembling seized her limbs and straightway the swordsmen drew their moon-curved blades. She cautioned them to stay their hands. Then to Ali she replied in a hoarse whisper, "Get thee gone, thou weaver of carpets. Thou juggler of jargon! Get thee gone!"

Smiling in proud confidence Ali exclaimed,

"Yesterday but a carpet weaver, but on some bright morrow I shall bear to thee a Dream-Weaving which shall constrain thy lips to confess: ***'Man hath not made it; only madness could have done it.'*** *Yesterday but a spinner of jargon in doggerel rhymes; but cometh a day when I shall return to this palace and out-tell all gifted poets who gather here."*

Then all unmolested he withdrew backwards from his lady. He left her house with face towards the door by way of a foretoken of a triumphant return. Leonorina, from the portal of the palace, watched until he disappeared from view.

When the day morrowed, Ali and his fag, Ferista, set out, afoot, through the Gate of Heaven of the City of Ingdad to discover the fabulous lands the Turk had told of. They soon descried the thorn thicket of Dame Happy-Chance, lying on the desert like a cast-away coronet withered and sere. At the wicket gate of this thorny garden they approached the gourd woman, who was blowing long blasts on a ram's horn.

Ali saluted, *"Hail, Sister Miriam, I bring with me Ferista, my fag, who will share my adventures to the World's End."*

"Thy Ferista hath a faithful look. At the World's End may he be richly rewarded as thyself."

"Wherefore all this trumpeting?" Ali asked.

"I am calling my faithful beasts of burden who are to bear thee to the Cave of the Winds. They know the way there; they know the way back."

She pointed to some leather bags at her feet and continued, *"Here are flagons of water and pouches of food. These beasts know where to find their own forage and drink because many a time they have made this same journey. They shall preserve thy unaccustomed feet from stone-bruise and thorn-prick, for long is the way to the Mountains of the Moon, and weary and wild. Ye would have been foot-sore and far spent ere half the journey were made. Far better guides are these creatures of mine than those wind-blown spiders. Gather of the gourds that abound in that place, place them in bags on the faithful beasts and they will bear them to me of their own accord."*

Whispered Ferista, *"I fear this ill-omened old woman. She hath the flesh of a mummy, the rags of a beggar and a gab like the crackle of thorns in the fire."*

"Hush thee, Ferista, she is a sister of the Queen of Eutukia, the Land of Happy-Chance."

Promptly and proudly retorted the dame, *"Worthy wanderers, ye shall bless the day on which I favored you. And thou, courageous weaver, thou must enquire in the city of Eutukia for the dame they call Penelope and who is known as the Mistress of Weavers. She alone can tell thee how to find favor with my queen sister and also how to find the Shrine of the Robe."*

By this time the animals had arrived. One was an aged camel such as the caravans turn astray to die, and the other was a dejected donkey.

Hissed Ferista, *"I shudder at these loathsome beasts. I detect a most unearthly gleam in their hollow eyes. They are like the scapegoats driven into the desert and laden with curses intended for some ungodly tribe. We cannot trust to a curse for a guide."*

By now Miriam had tossed the bags upon the animals and to Ali she said, *"Thou shalt ride this camel who answereth to the name of Fortunio."*

To Ferista, she added, *"Thou shalt ride this donkey named Bellerus."*

"But one thing, only one,
I have learnt from the Sun.
The fire he first lit
In my soul-conscousness
Still burns and goes on."

— Ernst Rhys

"Know the glory of the sun to be wine which
illuminates the whole world. I penetrate the
clay and land all their living force,
I glide into the plant."

— Unknown

"A noiseless patient spider;
I marked where on a little promontory it stood isolated.
Marked how to explore the vacant vast surrounding,
It launched forth filament, filament, filament, out of itself.
Ever unreeling them, ever tirelessly speeding them."

— Walt Whitman

Chapter Four

The Goblets of the Gabalouk

n due time they sighted afar the Mountains of the Moon, a wall of tender mauve above the lion-colored sands of the desert. For a length of leagues they trailed along the base of this heaven-high range until they espied on the sheer side of a greenstone mountain wall a projection shaped like the head of a shark. When they entered the grateful shadow of this jutting stone Fortunio and Bellerus gave snorts of satisfaction and they sniffed and pawed among the masses of dried vegetation there. Here Ali and Ferista viewed a grisly milieu. Half buried in the sand-drifts and heaps of vegetation were the skulls and skeletons of man and beast, and to some of these bones clung mummied flesh. But a most astounding sight was a of solitary man, wan-faced and weary-eyed, sitting stoop-shouldered on a little hummock of sand and dead leaves, and wearing a tunic of faded purple.

Ali dropped from his dusty camel, saluted the man, then asked, *"What place is this?"*

Pointing straight overhead the stranger faltered in a feeble voice, *"The mouth of the Earth."* Ali beheld, at a height of many cubits, a black hollowness like the open throat of a shark, and into this mouth sucked in a stream of gossamer spiders. Thereby Ali knew it must be the entrance to the Cave of the Winds. Fortunio and Bellerus began to munch the gourds which they found half-buried in dead leaves and stalks and stems.

After Ali had revived the man with food and drink he said, *"I perceive thou hast the garb of a man of mark. I pray thee acquaint me with thy status and with the strangeness of this place."*

"I am indeed of princely mark."

"How cometh a prince to be forsaked in shambles such as these?"

"Forsooth, my horsemen and their steeds have perished a moon and more agone, leaving me to press my quest alone."

"What quest is thine?"

"Perfume! I seek a particular fragrance which is to be found up yonder in the Throat of the World. Now tell me who thou art – and wherefore here."

"I am Ali the Weaver, seeking to concur with the world-weavers who gather anon in the Cave of the Winds. But tell why thou endurest the dangers of this fetid charnel house for a perfume."

"Since thou hast revived me in the face of approaching death I will inform thee somewhat of myself. I am the prince of a goodly land. But before I take my throne, my chair must be bossed with gem stones beyond compare, and my courtiers must wear the world's most noble odors; and before I make a queen of my beloved, I have vowed to present to her the most exquisite fragrance of the earth. All these rarities may be found up there in the hollow Mountains of the Moon. I am known as Agha Pha, the Prince of Perfume."

"O Prince Agha Pha I am but Ali of Ingdad, hither come to know the ways of fine weavings. But I, too, am on a quest for a perfume to present to the damsel of my heart's desire. I and my faithful fag, Ferista, were guided hither by these unpretentious beasts which serve Miriam of the Thorns and which are to return to her freighted with gourds from this place. O worthy prince, instruct me in the virtues of the essences thou seekest here."

"Worthy weaver, misfortune and a noble quest bind us into a brotherhood. Thou seekest gourds. Here groweth a miraculous gourd vine – the Gourd of Jonah. This is the season when that vine will issue from the Mouth of the World down to where we are standing. It hath leaves large as banners and blossoms large as trumpets. From these flowers drip the essence known as the Odor of Adventure, one of the Seven Perfumes of the world. This vine groweth to its fullness in a single night, but at the sunrise it faileth and falleth to the earth because a certain grubworm feedeth promptly on its roots. First we gather of that perfume then, with the vine as a ladder, we climb to the mouth of the cave. But a danger awaiteth us there. Should we find no favor with the winds of the cave, they would spew us from the mouth in a tempest of rage. Behold these skulls and bones here – unlucky wights who found no favor."

"I have a tutelary wind and a potent wish-word to protect us all. But who hath so instructed thee in the nature of this cave?"

"The Astrologer-in-Chief of my father's court, a man of transcendental knowledge. When we are safely in the cave I will enlighten thee as to the nature of the place."

Came the twilight hour that dimmed the desert and soothed the winds to rest. While the daylight darkled Ali and the prince discoursed concerning the cave and the manner of gaining entrance there. Said Agha Pha,

"No man knoweth the hour when sprouteth the vine of the gourd, but there are certain prayers and incantations to hasten its awakening. However, I have filled night after night here uttering unanswered prayers."

Came the late hour when the darkness seemed most solid, and when the myriad stars took their appointed places in heaven. While Prince Agha meditated as to what prayer to offer, the voice of Bellerus bellowed into the night with resounding brayings – with his snout uplifted towards the cave mouth relentlessly he brayed. The mouth of the cave responded with a glow of inner light. The beast silenced. The tip of the giant vine protruded and grew downward bearing golden buds that awoke into blossoms exhaling pollen dust and a most uncommon fragrance. The long vine kissed the earth and serpentined along the ground. All around its honied flowers flitted gorgeous moths on velvet wings. These were the moths that grew from the grubs that devour the roots of the vine, and their bodies were luminous like fireflies.

Cried Agha Pha, *"Haste thee, Ali! Haste thee! Catch the nectar now or never! This is the Odor of Adventure and it will endure upon thy person all thy days."*

Promptly Ali filled a gourd phial in his belt. As the vine cascaded in prodigious growth it shed gourds of sundry shapes and sizes which showered all around. Hastily did Ali and Ferista fill the saddle bags with random gourds and flung them to the backs of Fortunio and Bellerus who kept crunching the succulent leaves and stems of the vine. As soon as the beasts were laden away they went towards the Crown of Thorns.

By grasping of the leaf stems the three men upclomb to the stony lip of the Mouth of the World. Then up a slippery slope they crawled to the threshold of the cave. There they stood awhile in wonder. The roots of the vine were now eaten by the grub worms and immediately the massive trunk and branches avalanced over the lip of stone and fell to earth with horrid crash. The men stared into the monstrous maw of the Mouth of the World – a vastitude with no limits – with no need of sun or moon for it was all softly luminous with blue-green light which seemed to come from nowhere like the light in a dream. From overhead depended inverted pinnacles of vitreous rock studded with precious stones which shone with an inner fire, and some of these pendants tapered into slender tips like the fingers of a lovely hand, and some of these tips held peaches or plums or pomegranates all fashioned in colorful stones. The wind-worn walls were embedded with gems large and small, and the floor of the cave had windows of gem-stones etched from the walls. Some of these stones were large as melons, hollow inside and rattling with jewels when shaken, and some were of the size of cherries or myrtle berries or kernels of rice. There were bowers of primal plants bearing perfumes that were never abroad in the world, and amid these bowers were birds and butterflies on strangely beautiful wings. There were highways and pathways winding into unfathomed depths of the Mountains of the Moon, and there was a muted music like the combined tones of multitudinary wind harps – the Song of the Winds – the Music of the Spheres.

All unchallenged the men strolled athwart this realm of mingled blue and green and violet towards a far off glow of golden light. As they proceeded through the exotic gardens Agha Pha explained, *"Consider these wondrous waxen flowers. They are the Ideals of the common flowers of the world; and above them flit the Ideals of the butterflies, and among these branches are birds plumed as was never an earthly bird."*

"Region of Ideals!" exclaimed Ali, "Then this must be the Dreamland of which my father envisioned."

"Verily this is a Cave of Dreamland."

"Then I may meet the Moon Girl here."

"But Ali, the world hath many a cave and dell of Dreamland. Some are in the highest mountains, some in the depths of the sea, and some are in the dark dells of sacred groves. Earth hath many a hollow cave of dreams. How else could earth be so fed on dreams?"

"Whence cometh this thy knowledge of Dreamland?" asked Ali.

"From the High Astrologer in my Kingdom of Perfumes. He knoweth by rote all the lore of dreams in the sibylline leaves."

When they attained to the golden gleam before them they found that it came from a grotto which was as a balcony looking into an amphitheater – vast and high-vaulted –crowded with troupes of revelous men and women, of light-footed maids, seraphic and jubilant, and of noble-bodied men, young and old, and of white-bearded priests and raven-haired priestesses from sibylline oracles.

Cried Ali, *"What tempestuous throng is this?"*

"Thine eyes behold the Ideals of the Winds gathered for a carnival. It pleaseth the winds to disport themselves here in human shape because, in all the world, there is not bodily form more beautiful or more noble than the human male and female which God hath made in his own image. Before thy very eyes just now are the Ideals of the Winds – the thunder-voiced tempest that cleaveth the forest and the bacchanalian whirlwinds that dance girdled with lightnings and the drowsy winds that whisper of love in mad midsummer nights."

While the prince discoursed in this wise, Ali contemplated the Ideals reveling in garments thin as cobwebs.

They soared and dived and swirled and raced. At times a pair of Ideals would leap into a mutual embrace and spin with a rapture such as is seen in spirals of whirling snow on a windy, wintry day, and then some other couple would steal away from the riot, soft and slow as the cool vapors that flow out upon still waters in summer midnights.

Continued Agha Pha, *"Consider those roaring Ideals over yonder – black-faced and fire-eyed. They are the Winds of Fury – the terrible tornado, the sea lifting typhoons, and the mountain rending hurricanes. And now look! Those unsavory forms slinking through the throngs are the Ill Winds that never blow good. And now behold! Mingling with the revelers and halting their motions is the Clown and Jester, the Breathless Wind that becalmeth the sea and known among men as the Doldrums."*

On a sudden the windy throng fell into frantic jubilation. A commanding personage had attracted their attention. A halo of fire was round his head, lightnings flashed from his eyeballs and he waved a mighty scepter in his hand. Loud the wind-throng roared. *"Hail Aeolus! God of Winds! World-wandering Aeolus! Hail!"*

Hastily Prince Agha whispered, *"Be that our signal for departure. No mortal dare see or hear that wind-god, for the lightnings of his glances blind our eyeballs and the thunder of his speech burst the eardrums."*

Promptly Ali, Ferista and the Prince turned from the carnival and set out for the grotto of the Gabalouk, following the lead of the gossamer spiders which were trailing overhead. After long wandering through devious pathways they came to the cave of this wind-god.

Said the prince, *"I fain would see this cave, for at this season the Ideal of the Spiders, cometh here. Arachne is her name. She is an enchantress of slender grace, web-garbed and girdled with a silver belt set with cold jewels silver-bright. She is mistress of the myriad spiders whose tribes are silent as the silvery stars. And also cometh here the Ideal of the voiceful insects, the singers of the day and night. She is a damsel of delight and Moussia is her name in Dreamland."*

They entered into a mighty chamber all overarched with sleek greenstone and hung with long, gray, cobweb banners in which large-bellied spiders were pendulous like leaden beads. At the far end of the chamber a lofty alcove had been wind-bored into the stone wall. On the floor of the alcove was a stately throne-chair carved from the native stone. Back of this seat was a little curtained doorway in the wall. Suspended from the ceiling, and just in front of the top of the alcove, was a canopy, a wizardry of weavings by the Geometric Spiders and fashioned with lines and angles to bewilder the eyes and daze the imagination. Amid the webberies of this canopy, and like varicolored jewels, the parti colored Geometric Spiders hung. On either side of the alcove was the mouth of a tunnel tall enough to admit a mounted horseman, and there were other cave mouths all around the hall.

Directly to this alcove Ali led the two men. He halted before the vacant chair. Straightway from both tunnels appeared a great spider large as a sea turtle – black and bristling, electric-eyed and fanged like the dread tarantula. On either side of the alcove these horrifying creatures stood silent as shadows. Unmoved by these monstrous attendants Ali, in loud voice, acclaimed, *"Hail Gabalouk! Genius of the winds of fortune! A god-son of thine is here to hail thee homage. Hail Gabalouk!"*

At these words the spiders toddled back into the tunnels. Then in the depths of the tunnels a distant thunder awoke and it increased in sound as it seemed to approach. The thunder ceased when from the door back of the chair strode forth a young man, admirable of limb and body, fair of skin, ruddy-faced, blue-eyed, and with blond hair bushy and abundant as the mane of a lion. His only garments were of pelts of wild animals clapped about him, and a short-bladed sword, sheathed in rawhide, hung from a heavy waist-band. Impatiently he stood just in front of the throne-seat. Impetuously he challenged, *"What knave of fools hath dared my sanctuary at the hour when the conclave of the weavers is gathering?"*

"I am Ali, the Weaver of Ingdad, whose only wisdom is that he knoweth himself to be a fool."

"What seekest the fool in this chamber?"

"To consider the ways of the weaving."

"Go to the spiders for that. I am no spinner or weaver. But what seekest thou of me?"

"Puissant god of the fortunate winds, direct me to the fountain of wisdom which is the Well at the World's End, and from which I may learn the Saying that Sings."

"To trust a fool with that saying would be to trust a child with fire. The Saying that Sings is one of the world's Purpureal Powers and one which is reserved for the well-born and the high-minded. Only the temerity of a fool would ask for such an honor."

"O Gabalouk, my nativity was under a signal assembly of proud stars, and my craft of weaving shadows of dreams into textures is not one for a low-minded churl."

The Gabalouk took seat. "Why cravest thou this Saying, and for what usage?"

"Therewith could I subdue the mockeries in those soul-enthralling eyes of my beloved Leonorina, and I could gainsay the railleries of her tuneful tongue."

Like the roar of a wind over wide waters came the

response of the Gabalouk, *"He who seeketh wisdom to confound the unwise is not worthy of wisdom. And what is thy beloved more than another's beloved that I should so favor thee! Fool of fools! I will have none of thee."*

The Gabalouk rose as to depart; the spiders made as though to spring.

Then Ali threw up his arms and cried, *"Stay thee, O Gabalouk, genius of the streaming star, hear my plea.* ***Bélhamarámara****!"*

As though stung by a scorpion the wind-god halted. Slowly the two great spiders backed into the tunnels silent as the shades of death. The Gabalouk resumed his seat and in altered tones replied, *"Presumptuous fool! How came that wish-word in thy mouth? And what birth-stars were thine?"*

"I was born when the Sun was a guest in the House of the Lion, in the hour between the dawn and the sunrise, and when the Morning Stars were Jupiter and Venus, and when the crescent Moon was a bright boat between the two planetary fires, and at the moment when the wandering Star of the Gabalouk streamed athwart this celestial concourse. The wind of the Gabalouk shook the house where I was born."

The whole cave trembled with a touch of earthquake as though in confirmation of the words of Ali.

"Knowest thou that I am the Wind Genius of a fool's good luck?"

"Aye verily."

"Who told thee that?"

"The Sultan of Dreams, Zoumi Aazou, the teller of tales. He told me to follow the gossamers even to this shrine."

"The Turk is the Grand Prime Liar of the world. He sendeth fools wandering to empty lands at the end of the

world. Yet in all his tales a truth is hidden for the elect who are alert enough to see. Thou hast constrained me to humor thy folly. What is thy wish?"

"To know where lieth the Well at the World's End, and to know where dwelleth the Moon Girl."

"Fools of the world blindly seek the Moon Girl and few are they who find. To grant thine asking would be to confer upon thee one of the Purpureal Powers of the world – a crown too heavy for thy foolish head. Fool! – to ask for wisdom just to bewilder a foolish maid! There are two other Purpureal Powers which are far more potent over fickle damsels and far more easy for thy winning. The names of the Powers are these: SOVEREIGNTY, LOVE , and WISDOM, and the last of these is the hardest of all to win."

"Grant me to know the wisdom that sings."

"O weaver of Dreams! Child of the Lion! Favored of the crescent moon! Star-endowed! – yet but a fool yearning for the Moon Girl! Thou must learn how the starry Lion sought to woo the Moon and why he failed to find her. Untutored child, thou art at large with the torch of a wish-word which doth constrain me to grant one of the world's firebrand powers. Since I am to favor thee thou must bind thyself to my service and be ready to respond to whatever wish I may put to thee."

"My fealty to thee, O god of the Streaming Star – wind-god of fortune! On my soul I vow my service to thee now and ever afterwards."

"The paction between us hath been spoken."

All the webberies of the cave waved uneasily and their spiders fixed fire-eyes on Ali. Continued the wind-god, *"In homage to the great star Jupiter, sovereign of all the winds, and in deference to the Celestial Leo, and in adoration of the Love Star, Queen of Heaven, I will now arrange before thee here upon a table of stone three crystal goblets, each filled with a draught of one of the Purpureal Powers of the world. Fill thyself with the ichor of thy choice."*

Then he called out, *"What ho! Bring forth the table of stone and arrange it with the three Goblets of Fate."*

At his bidding appeared three silent dwarfs from a place behind the throne and bearing a table top and supports which they set before the alcove. The table was a slab of marble, grey with age, and in shape very like a tombstone recovered from some forgotten grave. Across this stone they flung an old spider-grey scarf which might have been a shroud ravished from some old sepulchre. Then the dwarfs withdrew to return with the three goblets which they set upon the shrouded slab. One goblet was filled with a wine that gleamed like molten rubies; another was filled with a golden hydromel sparkling like liquescent opals; the third held clear cold water of such a lively, pearly lucency that surely it must be from the Well at the World's End.

Said the Gabalouk, *"These goblets hold three embodiments of divine attributes. Choose but one. Quaff of the red wine and thou canst fill the mind of any man with fear. Fill thyself with the golden hydromel and thou shalt fill the eye of any woman with love. Drink of the water of the Pearl of Great Price and thou shalt drink the knowledge of the language of the insects. So now, mad-minded uninstructed oaf, thy wish-word hath constrained me to this offer. I have spoken. I leave thee to thy course of life. But time will come when I shall call thee to my service."*

With that he disappeared.

Ali strode to the table and lifted the goblet of wine. From the door behind the throne chair stepped forth a bland-eyed Persian satrap in festive robes of velvet and with a moon-curved sword at his side. He was fine of feature, elegant of stature and with soft hands burdened with jeweled rings. He saluted and salaamed and took seat in the throne chair to acclaim, *"Hail, Ali of Ingdad, high-favored of the Shooting Star! Child of the Lion, shielded by Jupiter! Choose for thyself now whether thou shalt be of the conquerors or of the conquered. The world is his who taketh."*

Holding aloft his scimitar he continued, *"Might makes right. Alexander built his empire with the sword. Pharaoh built pyramids with the flail. Choose now. Be thou a beater or a beaten? Quaff the blood-red wine of ambition and save thyself from the lot of a slave back-beaten by the stick of Egypt."*

Ali lifted the goblet of blood-red wine. Immediately the entire cave was bathed in rubescent radiance. All the grey hangings became tapestries of damask dye, and the leaden bodies of the spiders became as flaming rubies. The grey scarf of the table became a coverlet of purple velvet orfrayed with gold. From a tunnel appeared a procession of Turkish Pashaws and Sultans and Emirs and Grandees and Mamelukes and Officers of State with body-guards splendid with scimitars and with black slaves bearing salvers of silver heaped high with the tribute of conquered tribes. They encircled the hall to the sound of huzzas and trumpets while an ermine odor of the court of kings pervaded the air. In a side semi-circle they took their stand to acclaim, *"Ali of Ingdad! Drink the red wine and we will proclaim thee Ali the Great, Imperator over All."*

Ali, with goblet in hand, stood facing the pageant. Ferista whispered, *"Drink the red wine and save us from drudgery and servitude."*

Ali rejoined, *"Who ruleth by fear ruleth not the heart."*

He replaced the goblet untasted. The regal procession

withdrew into the opposite tunnel. The rosy light failed, the cave-light dimmed and once more the pendant weavings hung grey and leaden-beaded.

Next Ali lifted the goblet of hydromel. Slowly the light of the cave mellowed to the flow of a fire opal. The tapestries transformed into cloth-of-gold shot with carnelian beads fire bright as the gems in the belt of goddess Aphrodite. The coverlet of the table became a saffron velvet orfrayed with jetty black.

Beside the throne-seat then appeared a tall lady like a king's daughter, clad in clinging gown of white, gold-girdled, with long raven locks set with a tiara which bore a single gem star-bright and magic as moonlight. Proud and prudent she stood and with a compelling charm such as beseemed the far-famed Sorceress of the Nile. Said this queenly one, *"O Weaver of Dreams, favored of the star-queen Aphrodite, drink the drowsy hydromel and we shall make thy drowsy dreams come true."*

Out of the tunnel tripped forth bevies of damsels of such beauty as might bewilder Paradise, damsels made of musk and moonlight, houri-eyed and haunting, laughing and love-langorous, they tripped and danced sense-enthralled to secret rhythms. As they passed Ali they extended to him arms bare and braceleted, and in chorus they repeated, *"For our favors Kings and Caesars gladly toss a throne aside; for our favors many a Midas heaps his treasure at our feet. Oh lonely-hearted Ali, drink now the golden wine and we shall bear thee to the Island of the Moon – island of the love that lingers – island of the darts of joy – island of the thrills of passion – and in that isle we will proclaim thee Sultan of us all."*

With the hydromel in hand Ali stood transfixed by this pageant of beauty posed before him in the semi-circle of the new moon. He looked upon damsels with eyes cerulean as oriental heavens and with locks saffron as the stamens of the lotus, and with shoulders creamy as the petals on which the stamens loll. He looked also upon mysterious maidens, ivory-skinned and dark-haired as the midnight, silent and with black eyes of a terrifying beauty. Here were damsels with eyes of gazelles and voices of doves, and with a skin so soft and white that it must have been made of milk, and with lustrous locks of so subtile a scent that they must have been made of musk. But among this host Ali looked in vain for the Veiled One – She of hidden name – She of the moon magic – the guardian of the Day of the Bridegroom.

Ferista urged, *"Drink the hydromel. Choose for thyself a jeweled spouse endowed with seraphic beauty, and be envied by every man and woman in the world."*

"Who ruleth the eye ruleth not the heart. The eye is pleased with illusion but the heart boweth only to the beauty of truth," replied Ali.

He replaced the golden goblet. When the last beauty of the pageant disappeared in the tunnel the cave once more lapsed into a leaden-beaded greyness.

Ali lifted the goblet of water. The spider tapestries now transmuted to a gossamer silk of silver-grey starred with iridescent pearls which glowed like fireflies in a grey twilight, and these pearls were arranged in the patterns of the great Signs of Heaven. Among these pearls was one of transcendent lustre shining like the moon among the stars, and its name was The Pearl of Great Price. The coverlet of the table was now of a pearly silken gossamer bordered with azure and silver.

From behind the throne chair came now a maiden of faery grace and symmetry, clad in a tight fitting body robe of texture like the wings of dragon flies, a filamentous garment of a lustrous transparency and bespangled with moonglints of purple and gold. Her amber locks were free and floating and besprinkled with grains of star dust. Her eyes had the rich blue green of the sea.

Thus arrayed, she stood there fair as the finest creature ever made.

"O creature miraculous!" Ali said. *"Art thou the Moon Girl?"*

In a voice that was more of a song than a speech she replied, "I am called the damsel, Moussia. I am the ever living Ideal of all the winged fays men call flies. I am the frolic of all the dayflies, and the love song of the harvest flies, and the love dance of the fireflies. I am the wander-urge of the butterflies and of the daring dragon flies. And I share the delicious secrets of the voiceless midgets who have not yet taken on their wings.

"Oh Weaver of Dreams! I bid thee quaff of the Pierian Spring which sparkles in that goblet and thou shall attain to the language of the little fays I have named. They can tell thee secrets of the Earth, the Sun, the Moon and the Stars."

Ferista stayed the hand of Ali to exclaim, *"Shut thine eyes to this phantasmal Will-O'-the-Wisp. Stop thine ears to her persuasions. She is but an invitation unto madness."*

Ali growled, *"In a mood of madness Saul of Tarsus glimpsed the truth."*

Moussia continued, *"My creatures are the honey gatherers of the world. For them all flowers were created; for them hath every flower's fragrance been engendered. We steep our lives in all the honeys, and in all goodly savors. Before the Day of Adam we sang songs of love, and we spun and wove ere the Day of Eve. We were the first perfume gatherers; we were the first of weavers."*

Ali quaffed of the goblet.

Moussia commanded, *"Halloo! All ye Ideals of the*

fay flies! Come forth ye singers of the sunny hours! Spread here thy wings and have thy say!"

From the tunnel puffed an amber cloud of pollen dust which expanded throughout the cave and shed the basic perfume of all blossoms. Then appeared the Ideals of the fay flies on singing wings. More lovely were they than the many singing midgets abroad on earth. All their forms were much dilated. Some were faerie faced and some like elves and goblins. The Marechal of the Grasshoppers led the van. He took his stand to one side to review the passing pageant. In this swarming were cheepers from the tall green grasses, hummers from the marshes, hoppers from the dusty road-sides, golden-banded bees, hard backed clickers of castanets and myriads of cicadas mad with glee. At a signal from the Marechal they sang in chorus:

"Of all God's creatures we know best
the Song of Songs, and
the Song of the Sun, and
the Song of the Well at the World's End."

"O happy singers of the daytime! What is the Song of the Sun?" demanded Ali.

The Marechal of the Grasshoppers responded, *"The Sun is a ball of living fire. The Sun is alive and the Soul of the Sun is the spirit Uriel, whose fire is the life of all earthly sproutage and the life of all earthly flesh."*

The Chorus of Grasshoppers set up a chant:

"Hail Uriel! Life is captured sunlight
enmeshed in lovely forms.
Homage to Uriel, Soul of the Sun –
the breather of life into the clay of the earth.
Love is captured moonlight
enmeshed in beautiful dreams."

"O happy grasshoppers! Where is the Well at the World's End?"

"Where the sun shines hottest, happiest, there lies the Well. Hail Uriel! Where the rain clouds never darken, where the frost winds never deaden, there lies the Well, Hail Uriel! There lies the Well at the World's End, " chorused the grasshoppers.

"Tell me now the Secret of the Earth."

Replied Moussia, *"Ask that secret from the creatures that dwell in the ground – that delve in the earth. Ask the Satrap of the Scarabs and his hosts of scarabees to tell thee. Halloo! Halloo! Thou commander of the shining shards! Bring forth thy hosts to say the Secret of the Earth!"*

Then entered the Satrap, Scarabeus, with a vanguard of splendid scarabees such as were sacred in old Egypt. He stepped aside to review the incoming pageant. Following the vanguard came the horde of the beetle tribes –musical Musk Beetles with the perfume of old mummy robes – and the Moss Beetles – and the emerald Tiger Beetles – and the ebony Horned Beetles – and the gay backed Zoom Zooms – and the Click Clicks – and all the multitudinous swarms with particolored shards.

At a signal from Moussia the Satrap responded, *"The Earth is a Star, one of the Star Children of the Sun. The dust of the Earth is the dust of a Star. The dust of the Stars is the dust of the Firmament upon which God's footsteps fall. We are made of the dust of the Earth; we are the star dust that sings. We are the dust of the sandals of God."*

The Chorus of beetles chirped, *"We know what's under the ground. We know what's under the grave. We know what's in the bottom of the well. We eat the roots of the Gourd of Jonah; we eat the roots of the Tree of the World that grows by the Well at the World's End. We eat the roots of the grass of the graves in the shadowy groves in the Isle of the Moon."*

"Tell me of the Island of the Moon," interrupted Ali.

Scarabeus continued, *"In its sands are precious stones embedded. In its groves are many a mossy mound. In those sands that sing when trodden are treacherous sands that sink beneath the feet."*

The chorus of beetles clicked, *"We know well what lies below the singing sands of the Isle of the Moon. We know why the grass grows green on the mounds in the silent groves."*

Ali coaxed, *"Tell of the Well at the World's End."*

The chorus of beetles responded, *"Deepest of all wells it is whose waters rest upon the rocks of the firm foundation of the world. Darkest of all wells it is, whose waters mirror stars at noon."*

"And now," said Ali, *"Tell me how the Lion sought the Sickle of the Moon."*

Moussia, Ideal of the winged creatures replied, *"Ask that secret from the mistress of the twilight fays. Her cohorts know full well the Moon Girl, who flingeth tinseled moonlight over sullen stony lands, and who maketh stones to see and to sing. Come singers of the twilight. Come Lady Firefly and have your say!"*

Now came forth lovely Lady Firefly with her multitudes of lantern flies and will-o'-the-wisps and frail bodied phosphor bearers with no names. These light bearers were all a throb with darts of love, and all their song was of the moon.

With wonderment in his voice Ali addressed them, *"O phosphor bearers, unconfounded by the dark, wise to all the ways of moonlight, tell me what the Moon Girl's name is."*

"The Moon Girl," replied the Lady Firefly, *"hath a honied name; the Moon Girl hath a thousand names and she weareth the horns of the goddess Astarte. The Moon Girl walks with fairy feet that tread on the hearts of men."*

"How may I know her when she cometh?" breathlessly asked Ali.

"By a tide within thy breast," came the reply.

Then rose up a chorus of lantern flies: *"All around the Island of the Moon great tides uplift when cometh the Maid of the Moon. All round the singing shores the great Sea Ocean riseth up to kiss the Moon. So shall thy soul rise up in tide when cometh She, the Crescent-crowned, She with the light of the Moon in her eyes and the honey of Eden in her voice and the thrill of Paradise in her smile."*

With his voice filled with awe, Ali asked, *"Tell me of the Island of the Moon."*

Came the chorus of the lantern flies, *"It is a realm of rest and rapture; a land where nothing seems to change, where gorgeous beaches sing in sunlight, and in midnight shine like moonlight, and where pale flowers on long stems open fragrant petals by the side of alabaster tombs."*

"And where is the Well at the World's End?" demanded Ali.

The chorus continued, *"It is where the days are gladdest; it is where the nights are saddest. It is fed by tears that drop in sorrowing nights. It lies at the end of a long, long trail through a land of enchanted stones."*

Pausing briefly Ali again asked, *"O Lady Firefly, tell me of the quest of the Lion for the Moon."*

Softly replied Lady Firefly, *"The Lion of the Stars went forth to court slim-waisted Lady Moon. He has not found her yet. Ha! Ha! Not yet. Not yet. Ah, ha, ha, ha!"*

The chorus of the lantern flies rose up, *"When the Sun was a guest in the House of the Lion, and the Moon was afloat in the portals of the sunset, then the rays of the sun were the mane of the Lion, but the Lion in his glory could not see the Shining One singing in the sunset, and only She could tell the King of Beasts the Saying of the Tree of Knowledge. Thus the Sickle of the Lion sought the Sickle of the Moon."*

The twilight singers now withdrew and after them came the Singers of the Midnight. Came katydids and crickets and trillers from benighted caves, and clic-clic death-watchers and unnamed winged midgets who, at dead of night, sing of love beside forgotten graves. All these creatures in the rhythm of the crickets sang – in the beat of happy heart throbs – and their song was to the Star of Love, the great blue wandering Star of Hope, Star of Evening, Star of Morning, bright with duplicate horns, the Herald of the Day of the Bridegroom.

Lady Katydid led the van.

Ali addressed her politely, *"O Lady Katydid! Priestess of the shades of night, repeat to me the litany of the Day of the Bridegroom."*

Lady Katydid responded, *"The Sun is the Bridegroom; the Earth is the Bride; the Moon is the Bridesmaid; the Wandering Stars are the Sisters of the Bride; the steadfast Stars are the Wedding Guests; the Comet Stars are the Unbidden Guests; and the Twelve Houses in the Belt of the Universe preside over all."*

The chorus of katydids chanted, *"But only She, the Veiled one, the Shining One, can tell when cometh the Day of the Bridegroom, the day when the star-crowned Wedding Guests shall sit at feast under the Tree of Knowledge hard by the Well in the Waste."*

The Singers of the Twilight withdrew.

Ali turned towards the Ideal of the Winged Ones, *"O Moussia of the Midgets, where are they, the spiders, who are to tell the ways of finest weavings?"*

Moussia answered, *"The spiders are not the only webbers and weavers. There are many worthy websters 'mongst my fays. Thou shalt see and hear them now, and the Wazir of the Weavers shall inform thee of their ways. Halloo! Halloo! Ye chenille creatures! Come forth! For with us is a Weaver of Dreams whose god-father is the Gabalouk, the genius of the Shuttle Star which spinneth threads of silver fire athwart the Houses of Heaven."*

Straightway appeared hordes of larval creatures crawling on the ground, silk worms, cotton worms, cut worms, tent weavers, worms of the Nile, blind worms and worms of sundry kinds, and the Wazir of the Weavers led the van. This Wazir was a wooly wight much like a caterpillar. He threw aside his wooly coat and stood up in an elfin form, goblin-eyes, and wearing the cone-pointed cap of the fays.

In a loud voice the Wazir of Websters declared, *"Hail, god-son of the weaver among the stars! In homage to the Gabaloluk we shall favor thee."*

At these words each weaver-wight, as he crept by the Wazir, discarded his larval coat and rose upright and marched by wearing wings of moth or dayfly or dragonfly.

A chorus of Websters took up a chant, *"In larval days we had nor wings nor song, but our webberies were supreme of all earth's tissues. We wove the web of the veil of the Moon Girl; we spun the warp and the woof of the Master's Robe."*

Then said the Wazir, *"We toil, we spin, till we drowse into death-like sleep, knowing full well we shall wake to wings and to songs of love. Consider our faith, ye death-fearing mortals and be wise. Death is but a drowse from which we wake to wings."*

Ali responded, *"O Wazir I would fain be wise among the weavers."*

Continued the Wazir, *"First thou must know of the seven precious fibers of the world from which all finest fabrics have been woven. These are they: spinnings of the silk moth spun by moonlight, air threads of the gossamer spiders launched in sunlight, fibers of the finest flax grown in old graveyards, threads of satin spar, fine-spun wools from sacred animals, filaments of a glass made from the singing sands of the Isle of the Moon, and the exquisitely fine threads that are drawn from purest gold. These are the seven; and hereby I ask my websters and weavers to present to thee these filaments."*

From the parading pageant stepped forth certain members to place at the feet of Ali seven little bobbins wound with the Seven Threads.

The Wazir proclaimed, *"Do not demur to make withdrawals from these reels and bobbins, for the virtue of each thereof is this: the thread will restore its length in the measure that it be cut off, even as a silver thread is drawn without end from the spider's little body. Now as thou dost draw of this bobbin, the color of the thread taketh on the color of thy thought much as the chameleon's skin taketh the hue that happens in his brain."*

Ali secured these bobbins in secret pockets of his belt.

A chant from the weavers rose, *"We wove the web of the robe of the Moon Girl. We spun the thread of the robe which the Master wore on the day when he closed his eyes for a drowse of three days. Consider our ways and grow wise."*

Moussia now spoke softly, *"Cometh now the Epilogue of the pageant of the fays; cometh now those voiceless fays who shall never have wings, and who never shall sing. But these silent wights have much to teach thee. Halloo! Ye voiceless creatures of the underground, dwellers in the ooze and mire. Come forth and act out the life of every man."*

From the muddy lip of the mouth of a cave wriggled forth some silent sable creatures – elf things – water worms – coffin worms – and worms of conscience that begnaw the soul. Like the larval worms they threw off their uncouth coats and appeared as trolls who were deaf and dumb. Then with artful attitudes and gestures they performed in pantomime a play of signal significance.

At the end of the show they marched into a tunnel and when the last one disappeared Moussia declared, *"Here endeth all the pageant of the fay folks. O Weaver of Ingdad thy wish word hath summoned me to thy service. I have had my say. I leave thee to the spider folk."*

She withdrew with the retreating players of pantomime.

Agha Pha, the Perfume Prince asked quickly, *"What meaning shall we gather from the actions of these silent minstrels?"*

Spoke Ferista, *"It is but a dumb show for the dumb."*

Softly, Ali responded, *"It profoundly thrilleth me. This should be seen by every man – this portrayal of the inevitable conflict of the heart's desire with the will of the Fates. O what transterranean revelations have fed our ears and eyes."*

"And what soul-embalming perfumes," added Agha Pha.

"Yes. And what deliria of madness! What figments of fevers! We are entrapped in a bespidered sepulchre from which is no return. Folly following fools," spoke Ferista in an agitated voice.

Meanwhile the cave awakened with a gloomsome, vitreous, greenish glow. From overhead slowly descended great spiders with shudderous outspread claws. Forth from the tunnels reappeared those huge spiders more threatening than before. As each downdropping spider touched ground he doffed his skin and stood in his Ideal form, pleasant in face and figure and clothed in black velvet garnished with silver buckles.

This throng in velvet then importuned, *"Come forth,*

O mighty Mistress of Weavers, we, thy websters, are assembled here to disport before thee in all the ways of weaving."

From behind the throne chair appeared a strange lady with fascinating eyes of green and white cheeks tinged with rose. Her lustrous hair seemed of a fine-spun silver and it was banded with a diadem of silver set with pearl. Her milk-white arms were bare and braceleted with silver. The whiteness of her perfect body prevailed through the green of her gauzy gown and her waist, so slender-fine, was girdled with bangles of silver inlaid with gleaming emeralds. This hypnotic creature arranged herself with a winsome grace in the chair of stone and in a voice pleasing as the chimes of silver bells she responded to the greetings of the assemblage.

Then to Ali she said, *"O Weaver of Ingdad, vassal of the Shuttle Star. I have heard thy story here, and it findeth favor in my heart. Have thy say before me, and no weaver in this hall shall gainsay thee."*

Ali swept this vision with his eyes and exclaimed, *"O lovely lady! Art thou the Moon Girl?"*

"I am Arachne. By that name was I known when the goddess Athene, jealous of my weaving, in which she found no flaw, changed me into a spider. But now, through my myriad arachnids, I bespread the whole earth with my weavings far and wide. I bid thee now behold the ways of weaving which will take place here before thine eyes."

Promptly the Ideals of the spiders, in separate groups, danced for Arachne. Some performed on filaments drawn taut across the hall. In high trapeziums the acrobatic spiders twirled and dived and climbed, and the marvel of these surprising antics was this: each swinger left his acrobatic course traced out in a web whose tines and angles had all the harmonies of the action. Thus was the great hall soon festooned with laceries where patterns were as music to the eye.

At the end of the show the arachnids assumed their spider shapes and crawled back to the ceiling from which long, ragged weavings now hung hostile and thick-set as the mossy beards of some dark haunted forest from which is no egress. Once more in these filaments the spiders were inert as leaden beads. This grisly encasement affrayed Ali and his men and they disputed among themselves as to who could guide them hence.

Seeing their perplexities Arachne smiled, rose from her chair and said, *"O Ali, it as well that thou hast chosen the craft of weaving. It is well that thous hast followed the threads of my gossamers to this cavern. I will now direct thee to a certain thread which can lead thee hence. Come with me now to the yawning mouth of yonder cave which is called the Throat of the World."*

While Ali and his men accompanied Arachne she explained, *"The Cave of the Winds hath four great mouths facing the Four Directions and each entrance is beset with perils of its own. Few are they who find entry here and fewer are they who return, for among the winds is nor mercy nor sorrow, because it is not of their nature to know such human sentiments."*

They entered the Throat of the World and here Arachne plucked up a clue of silvery thread from which a filament led off into the unfriendly gloom. She extended to Ali the ball and said, *"Hold this clue loosely in thy hand, and as thou goest forward it will, of its own accord, reel the extended line into itself. This thread leadeth to a barge abandoned by a crew who, by the aid of witchcraft, entered the water mouth of this cavern in a craft well stored with food for a return journey. After they had cargoed their ship with jewels and perfumes which are to be found only here, and were ready to depart, they perished one and all. Moons ago their bones were spewed from the Shark Mouth of the cave. Trust thy fortune to this enchanted barge. Set it adrift in the tide. It will bear thee to the outer world. Fare thee well. Ali, Weaver of Ingdad, I have had my say."*

Chapter Five

Mouzaac and the Heart's Desire

The guiding silver thread led the three men through a tortuous trail dark and desolate and delivered them at last to the shore of a sable subterranean stream dark and cold as Acheron. Here at anchor was the enchanted barque. It was a cunning craft with a hull curved like the new moon, braced inside with stout tree trunks like unto the bamboo, and sheathed outside with heavy hides like those of the rhinoceros, and with silken sails hanging limp from tall reed stems. In the hold of the ship was found a storage of delectable goods such as cheeses, tubers of water lilies, dried fruits, candied gourds, rare honeys, crystallized beans and barley, and seeds of the lotus flower. There were bags and bundles of hastily garnered and unassorted treasure. In this uneasy barge the men went drifting towards a far off spark of light no larger than a firefly. As they approached this tunnel mouth the current quickened into slapping surges which threatened to crash the craft, and from beyond the tunnel mouth they could hear the muffled roar of many waters.

Suddenly, in a foggy daylight, they cascaded through spumiferous waves down and down until at last they shot into a broad bowl of blue water all rimmed around with verdures of divers kind, a paradise in a solitude bereft of human habitation. The sun of heaven gladdened their wild eyes. Behind them they beheld the cloud-white torrent spurting from the solid mountain wall of greenstone to quench its passionate unrest on the breast of this placid pool.

From this bowl of water the moonboat drifted with a noble river which serpentined through shadowy banks of ever-vernal foliage. After some days they descried habitations where people were indolent and dreamy and lightly clad, and who regarded the wandering boat with but languid interest. These clans had small need of toilsome tillage, for the trees bestowed pleasant fruits and nuts, and the shallows teemed with water plants that grew good seeds and luscious tubers, and in the limpid streams darted fishes of iridescent brilliance. These clans had small need of toilsome tillage so they beguiled their days with dances to soft music and with recitations chanted in tones of mild melancholy and everywhere an air of indolence and ease prevailed.

In due time the languid river delivered the moonboat into the harbor of a city by the sea. Around the river's mouth were wharves and piers. Most of them were neglected and deserted, and there were some vessels all moss-clad through long disuse. Across the bay gleamed a goodly city inviting to the eye. The boat touched upon a mossy pier whereon stood a solitary man with long gray beard and long silver hair. Ali hailed him, *"Who is keeper of this pier?"*

"It hath no keeper. It is to him who taketh. Moor thy barque here if so it pleaseth thee."

"What land is this?"

"Hedonia."

"And yonder city?"

"Lotophagia."

"Art thou a dweller of that town?"

"I have no dwelling place. I am an old sea captain without a boat. But tell me how you men happened with this dainty craft."

"We found the barge a derelict in the Cave of the Winds where the captain and the crew had perished."

"Perished! And such a lovely crew it was! Full many a moon agone this same galley sailed up this stream bound for the source of the river which is a mighty fountain leaping from the Mountains of the Moon."

"We found this boat all treasure-laden and provisioned for a return voyage. But tell us something of its crew and captain and tell us something of thyself."

"I am a seasoned mariner, Mouzaac by name, who knoweth nearly every port and every land, and who yearneth to escape from Lotophagia. This derelict which thou hast reclaimed came from the Island of the Moon. It was a festival season when it went by here. High in that moon-boat prow a regal woman sate and in the poop a black-robed woman endowed with witchcraft. From within that boat came the voices of women chanting to the beat of tabors so that neither the captain nor the crew might lust for landing in Lotophagia, for whoso landeth there careth never to return. This argosy dared all dangers to gain the Cave of the Winds and gather certain gems and jewels there. Though now the Island of the Moon is salted with jewels and sated with

odors yet there remain certain gems and perfumes which the empress hath not. Chief among the gems which she craveth is The Philosopher's Stone and chief among the perfume is the Odor of Isis."

In excitement Ali cried,*"By the Gabalouk! This boat may bear these very treasures in her cargo. I beseech thee, worthy mariner with no ship, be thou the captain of this craft. Pilot us to the Island of the Moon and restore these treasures to the empress ."*

"Knowest thou that isle?"

"By legend only."

"I sojourned there in my youth, I rejoiced that I survived to tell the tale thereby. Believe me, young man, it is an isle of sirens, and isle of counterfeit delight. Its singing sands hold many a pearl which grew from a tear dropped there. Among its many perfumes is one to drug the judgements of the wise."

Spoke up Agha Pha, *"Perfumes! I shall test them one and all and hold fast to what is good. I am proof against all dangerous perfumes. What other dangers are in that isle?"*

"The isle is girdled with reefs of rock infested with cocodrills, the great sea reptiles which leap even to the deck of a vessel to devour a seaman. Though thy feet gain those bright perfumed shores they may be swallowed by the hungry quicksands."

Said Ferista, *"Hedonia is a most delightful clime, with friendly and mild-mannered people, and yonder Lotophagia is a goodly town to look upon. Is not this land quite good enough?"*

"Hedonia seems good enough. Some prefer this land to any other, it seems. And for that reason one should shun the place. It is a land of day-dreams, a land of sweet idleness that steals away man's fiber ere he is aware. It is a narcotic anodyne to the cowardly fear of

living. Who dines and wines in Lotophagia cares to wander nevermore."

Ali continued, *"Since thou knowest all cities what sayest thou of Eutukia?"*

"I have been there. It is the city which guards the dice which the men cast for the Mantle of the Master, a city of games and gamesters and with lusty festivals for the eye and ear, but a city which starveth the heart. It lieth far beyond the Moon Isle. Easy is the voyage to Eutukia and every man is welcomed there."

"What sayest thou of The Well at the World's End?"

"Ah! I have heard of that Fountain. It lieth far over the great Sea Ocean at the utmost league from Lotophagia. The Well at the End of the Way. Ah me! Its waters may be the only earthly solace to my soul."

"We are thither bound. Be thou the master mariner of this ship which fate hath entrusted to our disposal. I am favored of powerful stars: of the Lord Star who ruleth the winds and the rains, of the Love Star who ruleth the Isle of the Moon, and of the Sickle of the Moon in whose honor this boat is bended. And I have also the good will of the Gabalouk, the Shooting Star, whose heavenly dashings are not to be computed by astronomer or astrologer. With such tutelary favors why should we harbor any fear? Let us all embark together."

Mouzaac added, *"Myself when young did flee my home to see this wide and wondrous world and find therein a land of the heart's desire, only to learn that heart's desire departed the place the day before I landed there. I have had the good fortune of home and family and worldly wealth and office of high degree, but satisfaction of the soul came not with these. Now, in my days of silver hair I find me hungry among the husks of life. And yet, all the while, a mysterious something pursueth me. In moments of world-weariness my soul doth half-welcome this Pursuer. Mayhap only in surrender may I find peace. Mayhap I might surrender at the Well at the World's End."*

Then he added in a hoarse half-whisper, *"Methinks I am pursued by HIM."*

Chapter Six

The Island of the Moon

In brief period Mouzaac persuaded a crew of seamen to the venture. With the little vessel well manned and provisioned they set off in an hour of night when the moon rose round and rosy, and by morn they were out on the broad dark sea. The ship seemed to sail of its own accord, like a migrant bird who knoweth whither bound; and gracious were the winds and tides.

Nine days and nights the crew swiftly sailed the great Sea Ocean without adventure. On the tenth day they descried in the distance a low dome of water rising above the ocean.

Announced Mouzaac, *"Yonder swelling in the waters hides the Island of the Moon. Around that isle the tide is ever high, and sometimes the waves do so upswell that they appear to hang upon the clouds. Our first adventure is to mount this water wall."*

When they gained the apex of these encircling waters

they beheld afar the splendid Island of the Moon, and over the waters a humid, honied odor came.

"Our next adventure is to pass the ring of hostile rock that protects the isle," he said.

They skirted the barrier reefs from which schools of dread cocodrills swam forth and trailed in the vessel's wake as though expecting one more wreck. Full many a wreck could now be seen on the pikes and pinions in the reefs. Mouzaac found a favorable entry through the reefs and this brought them into a view of the Honey Islands, a belt of little landscapes that girdles the Island of the Moon, and each islet hath a honey of its own. Beyond this perfumed belt they sailed into the broad embrace of a goodly harbor with a splendid city dimly seen in far distance.

As a strategem Mouzaac unfurled at a mast-head a pennant which was an emblem of the island. This started little squads of horsemen to gallop along the strand with friendly gestures. When the boat slowed down in a dying wind a skiff with swarthy oarsmen sped forth to signal where safe moorage could be made.

When Ali and his men came ashore a silence fell upon the natives, for they perceived that none of this crew was of this island. Thereupon strode forward a man of authority, a powerful fellow with rings in his ears. His hat was of military cut and his waist was bound with a robust belt of leather which held a broad-bladed sword. He demanded, *"What error is this that insults our shores? How come ye with this craft which flies an ensign of our empress? Pirates! Brigands! I am captain of the coast guard here. Give good account and speedily ere your blood be turned to rubies in this sand. Hear ye! Of late we have beheaded pirates in this very place."*

His swarthy body guards marched forward and stood beside him with drawn swords like those wielded by executioners.

Responded Ali, *"Worthy captain shouldst thou know me and my men thou wouldst greet us with palm branches instead of scimitars. I am restoring things that are thine. I found this ship a derelict and deserted. Over perilous seas I have directed to its native shores this barge all intact with its treasure-trove of precious stones and perfumes. I bid thee acquaint thy empress with this arrival."*

An expansive smile melted all ferocity from the captain's face and disclosed large gleaming teeth. *"Ah, ha! This will be a dainty tid-bit for the ears of our great Gloriande! And thou hast thereby an engaging tale to tell I ween?"*

"A tale to strain belief."

Quickly the captain thrust forth his huge hand in token of welcome. *"I bless thy landing! Our fastidious queen is highly fond of tales of daring, so methinks she will grant thee a hearing. Thy coming is quite fortunate for me. It hath been many a moon since I have brought to her an auspicious accounting. Forsooth, at my last report she dubbed me a Gleaner of Gloom and she bade me breviate my talk hereafter. But now! Ah, ha, ha. I have a tale to hold her heed and make her hungry for the expatiation. Methinks she may reward me with a better uniform and a higher office. Pray tell me something of thy self, young man, and of the recovery of the ship."*

Ali recounted his affair.

Replied the delighted captain, *"More engaging than I guessed! Thou hast a talismanic tale. She shall hear of this. Meanwhile thou and all thy equipage shall find shelter in my ample hostellerie until I learn the disposition of our queen."*

On the morrow the captain returned to his spacious encampment which he called his hostellerie. He exulted, *"Praise that I have lived to see this day! I have been promoted to the office of Wazir of the Court of Gloriande! The queen was so profoundly taken by thy tale that she will grant thee audience, not right away, but on our most magnificent gathering of the year, our annual Festival of the Moon. This event draws hither, and from afar, many folk of high degree. Imagine! Thou art to appear before the court of great Gloriande the queen! I am to have full charge of all that festal affair. Therefore, I shall garb thee and thy colleagues in costumes befitting the occasion. Abide here in my camp until cometh the day of the Festival. Meanwhile to beguile the tedium of waiting this event, and to divert thyself meanwhile, the queen hath assigned to thee a band of musicians, a group of acrobats, an astrologer, and a poet. They are at thy orders. Now, Prince Ali, pardon my hasty leave. I am much concerned with my new affairs."*

Ali found these musicians skilled with cithera and systrum and wind harp and tabor, and they awoke amazing moods with flute and flageolet. Straightway he instructed these men to render the song of the Winds as it came to him from the Throat of the World. These music men were of handsome face and noble form, but Ali marveled that all of them were blind.

Spoke their leader, *"Our eyes have been darkened by the moon-bright eyes of Gloriande. This hath saddened our hearts but sweetened our songs. Yet it is our high delight to sing her praises and bid her biddings, but our hearts are ever sad."*

Asked Ali, *"Why not flee the blandishments and bewitchments of this enervating isle and regain glad eyesight in the world of honest men?"*

"Oh! Would that our will-to-flee had the strength of

our will-to-remain! Better it were that some of the ruthless pirates, who came here, might abduct us in chains to a land of sane and sound mankind!"

"Hath thy queen such small compassion on anguished hearts?"

"Our adored queen feedeth on that sweet note of anguish in our song. Forsooth, our great Gloriande herself is at times stone-blind, and doth stare with eyes fashioned to reflect the stars but which are wells of Stygian darkness."

"I will instruct you in songs to bewilder the darkness of that eye-bright empress, and to win her heart to a loving pity for the souls she hath so tortured."

Ali found the acrobatic men were deaf and dumb. Gloriande had cast this spell of hush upon them because she cared naught for their ardent words of love. But now they expressed their love with their eyes and with meaningful movements of their agile bodies. Straightway Ali instructed them to perform in pantomime, the elucidation of how Fate and Chance deny the desires of kings and queens and subjects – the esoteric pantomime which was acted out in a dumbshow by the little voiceless creatures in the cave.

The astrologer was a man profound in the lore of the heavens. When he heard of the ruling planets of Ali's birth and of his tutelary shooting Star, he bowed his head groundward and declared, *"O Ali of Ingdad, rejoice thyself in that thou art so star guided in this world of blind and dumb and fool-following souls. But beware of trusting solely to the stars. Only through thine actions can they bestow their virtues. Sloth is death. Action invokes cosmic aid. Trust the Soul of the Cosmos. Act. And be not afraid."*

The Poet was a prince clad in velvet, soul-saddened through years of unrequited love for Gloriande, but sole-fragrant with lovely lyrics which he made for the queen's delight. His face was thin, his hands were long, and his eyes bespake a soul on fire. The Poet gladly took Ali on strolls through his favorite glens and glades where it was his wont to create his finest poems. He conducted Ali to his favorite cave which was not far from the gate of the hostellerie. He pulled aside the long mosses that curtained the entry and then Ali found himself under an inverted bowl of smooth hard stone. From the ceiling a tiny rivulet plashed into a pool in the moss-covered floor and awoke silvery, whispery echoes in the enclosure. When Ali marveled at the entrancing harmony of these blended echoes, the Poet exclaimed in joy, *"Thou, too, art a poet. Thou, too, hearest meanings in these cave whispers. I call this echo song: the Dream of a Love that might come true."*

Then he led Ali to a solitary little mirror lake enclosed with high walls of verdure. Said he, *"This is the Lake of Remembrance. Who drinks of these waters never grows old."*

From the center of this lake rose a high cone-shaped pillar of stone-and-earth, all mossy-mantled and ivy overgrown and set with many a slender cypress tree.

"I call this the Isle of Might-Have-Been but others call it the Little Isle of Green Sods."

To this islet he ferried Ali on a raft of reeds. Upwards they wended past little shrines carved into the rocks and overgrown with fragrant moss and shrubs. At the door of one shrine he plucked some waxen berries which he crushed in his fingers and then handed them to Ali who exclaimed, *"What odor is this? What solvent of the soul? It doth take hold upon my heart as though it would never let go!"*

The Poet laughed and answered, *"It is indeed a fragrance to haunt the heart till death. It is the perfume of a love that might have been."*

One night he led Ali to the shore to hear the sands sing in the margin between the high tide and the low, and to see the glow and glimmer of the jewel stones half buried in the beach.

The Poet pointed seaward and explained, *“See yonder white spume where the amorous tide spends all its ardor upon unresponsive sand. In that foam my beloved did disport one night. Then like goddess Venus she emerged and on these very sands, that twitch at the touch of her toe, she danced in moonlight. In memory of that light-footed white-footed dance these sands keep singing evermore:*

O sickle of moonlight declining
Reflected by desolate waters,
O sickle of silver, what dream-fashioned harvest
Is stirred by your gentle resplendence below?*

Then came the day of the Festival of the Moon when Ali should appear before the queen Gloriande. A large concourse of people had gathered around the palace awaiting the signal to enter the hall. The Wazir had constrained this throng to await the conclusion of a Ritual of the Moon which was taking place inside. When the sound of trumps and tabors announced the end of ceremonies the whole throng billowed towards the audience hall.

Somewhat like a mosque this chamber seemed, carpeted and faintly aromatic and with tiers of upper galleries packed with people in expectancy. From the apex of the inner dome a chain-dropped lamp was pendent above a pool, moon-round and rimmed with azure tiles. Reclining on tiled floors around the pool

*D'Annuncio

were bands of acrobats and jugglers and wrestlers and minstrels and of disporters of divers sorts awaiting their turn to entertain the sultana and her court.

The approach of Gloriande was heralded by a bevy of black-haired girls, high-breasted and silver sandaled, strumming harps or clicking castanets or clashing cymbals. With them marched swingers of censers which outstreamed vaporous scarfs tinged with ambergris and strong-scented musk. Then came a priestess leading her temple girls who were swathed cap-a-pie in robes of purple purfled with gold. The priestess repeated a ritual and announced the advent of the festivities, and the approach of the Illustrious One.

The whole assembly rose to the acclaim of many voices and to the strumming of many strings. In she came glorious with golden-hair and great blue eyes and surrounded by handmaids with raven locks and golden gowns and white feet in silken saffron sandals. She stood with arms uplifted and from her bracelets drooped chains of gold which fastened to her girdled waist. Then with supple ease she seated herself in a chair of gold moulded into the shape of a shell. She seemed a personage all of gold - a vision to dazzle the eye and captivate the heart and confound the wits.

Promptly the Wazir of Ceremonies signaled all the actors to their roles.

There were tumblers and wrestlers and sword-dancers and lithe little acrobats who seemed without bone or bodily weight. There were clowns in tumid dress, and jesters and minstrels in motley. There were lion-tamers who gamboled with the growling beasts, and there were fire-dancers in veils diaphanous as vapors, and who danced amid flames high as their heads. In the great pool under the dome a troupe of girls with milk-white skin and green-dyed hair, rendered a Mermaid Dance.

They dived and swam and disported themselves with shouts of joy which echoed in the blue vault overhead, and each one lovely as a slice of the moon.

To these performers, all and singly, Gloriande tossed bracelets or bangles or wroughton trinkets or coins of the realm according to the merits of the show.

Proclaimed the Wazir, *"Cometh now a teller of tales – raconteur – who hath prevailed over all dangers that bristle in perilous lands. He hath a tale whose like hath never before been heard. But ere he speaketh I have some worthy men to testify concerning him. First let us hear from our Court Astrologer."*

The Astrologer approached and said, *"Our destinies are all recorded in the stars at our birth. This man is favored of the great wandering stars, Jupiter and Venus, and of the steady star which is the Eye of Leo. He is endowed with the courage of the Sickle of the Lion and therefore he hath the daring to court the favors of the Sickle of the Moon. With all these star-dowers he is a foundling of Lucifer, the Quicksilver-Star, who darteth through the Houses of Heaven in a course not to be charted by Astrologer or Star-Watcher. Surely such a starry equipage will lead its fondling to some bright destined end."*

After the applause subsided the Wazir proclaimed, *"I now request our Court Poet to inform us of this man."*

Arrayed in princely garb the Poet Prince stepped forth, bowed to the multitude and said, *"This raconteur doth think in words of music. Hear now what he hath accomplished with the blind musicians who now cometh forth. He hath instructed them to render the Song of the Winds which he learned in the great Cavern in the Mountains of the Moon."*

Entered the blind musicians who with their instruments contributed a harmony like the Music of the Spheres. To the rhythm of their instruments they recited a song of such love and longing that Gloriande unconsciously rose from her golden chair.

Then came forth the Wazir, *"Cometh now a band of men who can neither speak nor hear. Yet he hath instructed them in a pantomime to interpret the struggle of the heart's desire against the ways of Fate."*

Then entered the agile dumb acrobats and in pantomime they so perfectly acted out their roles in such strange and rhythmic motions that the face of Gloriande, erstwhile so enraptured, now darkened with the tragic truth of the voiceless show.

Then the Wazir announced in loud voice, *"Cometh now the man himself."*

The Wazir had tricked out Ali as a Turk with a turban of blue and trousers of saffron, and coat of embroidered cloth-of-gold and with jeweled slippers turned up at the toes. From the great assembly came echoed cries, *"The Turk! The Turk!"*

Ceremoniously the Wazir led this Turk to the appointed spot in front of Gloriande. The Turk salaamed and saluted and to Gloriande he addressed, *"Exalted empress! Enthraller of hearts! For whose favors potentates have gladly thrown aside a kingdom, I am by craft a wandering weaver bent on knowing all the wondrous weavings of the world. By the wiles of Fate I am constrained to appear before thy splendid personage. I bless the hap that hath placed me here before thee."*

Graciously the empress responded with words of greeting and bade the weaver have his say.

"My errand to the Island of the Moon is to restore to its empress an argosy long lost in the Cave of the Winds, and freighted with the potent jewels and perfumes which I hope may grant blandishment to the heart of great Gloriande. I shall now recount a tale whereby I have gained entrance to the Cave of the Winds, and

have plucked from the throat of the maw of danger these multiple measures of treasure. Lo! Here cometh that which is thine."

At a signal from Ali in marched a procession of Arabian slaves bearing on their heads salvers of silver, high-heaped with the treasures rescued from the cave. They arranged these salvers at the feet of Gloriande. The vast hall resounded with long hosannas and the great white lion roared.

Then Ali, in words which of their own accord seemed to flow from his lips, recounted a tale the likes whereof the empress Gloriande had never heard. She was entranced by this bewildering Tale of the Turk.

Then to the audience she called, *"What recompense is fitting for this master of musical words who hath dared to pluck the treasures from the jaws of danger?"*

Then someone shouted, *"Make him sultan of the Island." Then all at once they cried, "Make him Grand Sultan of us all!"*

Then broke forth such tumult that with difficulty could the Wazir restrain them, and some of the cheering throngs that pressed upon Ali had to be beaten back with staves.

"He shall be honored in our banquet hall tonight where noble men and women may hear his tales."

The show was now over.

That very evening in the Banquet Hall high on the terrace Ali sat at feast beside the queen, by merit raised to that envied eminence. Among the guests were Grandees and potentates of far lands. And with them were their dames. It was a festival of rare scents and savors. With the scent of wine and women were blended the fragrant vapors that rose from braizers redeemed from old temples of forgotten gods. It was musical with sweet-voiced girls who chanted hymns to Isis and Lyrics of the Moon. It fed the eye with a dainty dance performed on a festooned dais by damsels clad in the old Egyptian style. And all the while cup-bearers, supple as wands of willows, kept serving drowsy wines.

At the height of this pleasantry, Gloriande whispered, *"Prince Ali, wilt thou not make brief escapement from this overzealous throng and walk with me to where I may look upon the moon?"*

They strolled athwart the terrace garden – a parterre of Paradise all moon-litten and blossom-scented and musical with the lisp of fountainous waters. They rested their eyes upon the stars in their constellations and discoursed concerning their influence upon mankind. They serpentined through leafy boreage and out upon glades of grass bediamonded with dew.

At last they reached the rim of the cliff and in full view of the sea. At this place a narrow foot bridge was suspended like a spider's web from the cliff to the flat tip of a pinnacle of chrysolite in the sea. As they entered upon the bridge it undulated beneath their tread until they stepped forth on the flat top of the column planted in the waves. Here was a moon-curved bench carved out of the chrysolite. Gloriande motioned Ali sit beside her and there in silence they faced the splendid plumes of moonlight on the sea.

"Prince Ali, wise in thy world wanderings, dost thou know the Exhortation of the Moon?"

A chill shivered his frame at the mention of this litany which he could in no wise recall. Coldly he replied, *"I know it not."*

She sighed, *"I would that someday someone could repeat to me that esoteric saying. Each and every year on this occasion and in this place I contemplate the moon in silence hungry for the saying which fathoms the mystery of the Moon."*

"She is making merry mockery that I am unable to repeat the exhortation to the moon." Ali gave vent to nervous laughter and the queen herself joined in. Then they laughed together while the moon made grotesque faces on the tide.

She rose and stood in the enchanting beauty of the veil of moonlight. She saw the fascinated gaze of Ali's eyes.

"My people have commanded thee to abide with us on this isle."

"O Empress of the Moon Isle, I am sworn to a pilgrimage to the Well at the End of the World beyond a land of far distances there to commune with the Stones that See and the Stones that Sing and with the Stone of Silence. Only in that way may I attain to a wisdom worthy of thy hearing.."

"Ah me! How long the way to that well and how wild! And what availeth the wearying words of wisdom when the apple of thy heart's desire hangeth here within thy grasp? Tell me, dear Prince Ali, is not love worth more than wisdom?"

Here she stood a phantom of infatuation. Ali covered his face with his hands. Inwardly he raged that he could not repeat the litany of the moon which was laughing at his plight.

She saw his deep disturbance. Lightly she touched his shoulder and said, *"Keep thine answer for another night. The half minute glass of our tryst hath spent its sand. Let us back to the banquet ere the gorging crowd takes note of our departure."*

On the morrow while Ali, in the seclusion of the hostelry, was diverting his fancies with his musicians and his acrobats, there came a herald from the Palace to announce a great banquet of the Moon spread for all the people under the bowers near the palace. Places would be prepared for Ali and all his crew and comrades. Then the herald placed in Ali's hand a little sealed missive in the queen's own handwriting. It requested him to bring to the feast the white dove that disported among the flock which was caged in the hostelry.

After Ali read this missive a tumult throbbed his heart and head and he became quite beside himself. He quit the roistering noises of the camp and for refuge he fled to the soothing solace of the moss curtained cave. There he reclined on a bower of moss and listened to the whisperous waters until he fell asleep. Then the things of dreams took place before his eyes – divine Ideals of Dreamland and among them he beheld the Ideal of the face of Gloriande. Awakening, he felt in his belt for the bobbins of threads which the weaver worms had given him in the Cave of the Winds. With miraculous speed his fingers threaded in silken filaments a portrait of the Ideal of Gloriande, a dream picture with a halo of golden hair and a star and a crescent above her brow.

Came the night of the festival. Ali was carried to the palace in a paliquin from Hindustan borne on the shoulders of black slaves appointed by the chamberlain. To Gloriande Ali presented the white dove which was bound to his wrist by a silken cord, and he presented the dream likeness of her face glorious with golden hair.

Gloriande contemplated the weaving. Ali stood in awe and silence while she spoke, *"This seems a portrait of my soul – of my better self. Thou wizard of weaving."*

Night came. There was a riot of revelry around long tables spread beneath grateful greeneries whose branches were fruited with paper lanterns of divers colors. There were viands to daze the wits – camel colts and gazelles roasted whole – sherbets of many hues – colocassia roots toasted in honey and heavy wines of noble savor; and above the boisterous voices was the throb of tabors and drums and trumps.

A brace of boxers fought with naked fists, a Cambodian maid performed a languid dance while girdled with a python which embraced her dark torso. Then in ran a group of nimble-toed Circassian girls to dance to the tambourines thumped by albino maids.

Then softly spoke Gloriande to Ali, *"O thou weaver of dream faces – weaver of music for those who are blind – weaver of silent rhythms for those who are voiceless – thou hast won the heart of my people. They bid thee tarry here with thy songs and thine entrancing pantomimes."*

The lips of Ali remained close pressed. Then she touched her light fingers to his shoulders and she whispered, *"Let us escape from this loud merriment. Just you and I. Let us see once more those pantomimic faces on the nearby sea. Already the hour of moon rise is at hand. Haste thee."*

She cast the silken shawl from her shoulders. Their path led through a sable grove where murmurings of strange night birds and aromas of balsamic boughs lulled the senses to agreeable non-resistance. No word she spake and Ali heard the tingle of the little golden bells that graced her ankles.

They gained the belt of the singing sands. Silently she turned her steps to the diaphanous bridge. Silently followed Ali. Once again on the cliff they descended a narrow trail to the silvery sands below. Facing the moon they strolled the beach where self-luminous stones made here and there drowsy gleam and Ali marveled that each step of Gloriande left a faintly radiant footprint which softly crooned.

"O weaver of silent rhythms, thy pantomime players have inspired me to a new dance set to the music of dreamland. Thou shalt be the first to behold this rhythm."

Straightway she began to dance. Round and round she capered until her radiant footprints described a circle on the sand. Then in the center of this circle her figure swayed and pirouetted tip-toe with tinkling anklets until a flow as of smothered embers awoke beneath her feet. Still she danced on, she the great Gloriande, clad in her banquet robe of thinnest lawn like unto those scarfs of rainbow which her fire-dancers flaunted. She was a golden vision, filamentous and fanciful, conjured out of some wine-drowsy dream. Then she stood above that fire-dish which sang in sweet applause.

Whispered Gloriande, *"Am I not the Moon Girl? Am I not the great She who flingeth magic over stormy sands? Who maketh stones to see and sing? Am I not the heart's desire?"*

In silence Ali covered his face with his hands.

"O Ali, thou art the Stone of Silence. Mirror my heart to me in words of sweet affirmation."

Ali remained trembling and voiceless.

"At another time then thou shalt return to this very place at this very hour and answer me. See! These sands glow golden where we stand. For a whole moon thus will they glow and sing in remembrance of our meeting."

"When may it please thee that I return? By what portent may I know?"

"I will release the white dove. It will return to its perch in thy lodge. By that signal thou must come to this very glow in the sands at this very hour when the approaching night starkeneth the daylight."

"I shall honor the summons of the white dove," Ali answered.

Just then discordant tumult in the distance hushed her voice. She stood in alarm *"I mistrust our banquet hath fallen into some unhappy issue. We must cut short this tryst of ours but we must return."*

In a brief time she rejoined the banquet. Her commanding voice and her uplifted arms brought quiet to the mob that was turbulent around the tables all overturned.

Promptly Ali gathered with him Mouzaac and Agha Pha and Ferista and all his train and marching well in order they returned to their camp. But never a word of this royal tryst did Ali betray to any of his comrades.

Everything in this world is only a shadow
of what is an imperfect image of the Eternal.
Life, then, is a shadow..... This world is only Shadowland.

— *Unknown*

The world is a mirror of the soul.
The soul is the mirror of the world.

— *Unknown*

In the late afternoon of a long day the white dove returned to Ali's lodge. All unobserved by his comrades he stole quietly from the camp and directed his course towards that mystic beacon buried in the sand. When he arrived there a darkness deep and silent held all the forest that bordered the shore. He reached the rim of the moon-round plot of sand, but for him it seemed too sacred for his tread. So he stood there in the glooming light. Out of the forest appeared the white figure of Gloriande approaching silent as a ghost. He could hear the beating of his heart. She was approaching. He awaited motionless on the rim of the glow in the sand. She stood a moment gazing into the eyes of Ali. She was wrapped in a robe of fine white wool and girdled with gold at her waist. Her long loose golden hair was bound at the brow by a circle of jet, and her cheeks had a tinge of rose. Her beauty needed no foil of the lapidary, and no embellishment of the broiderers, and no trickeries of the hair-binders.

In quiet tones she said, *"Prince Ali, truly thou art of noble mien. Thine eyes are two dark wells of wisdom."*

She drew forth a round mirror of polished bronze and said, *"Behold thyself as thou art."*

"What witcheries! What magic is in this mirror? I do behold my features transformed into the aspect of a demi-god."

She laughed and answered, *"This is the mirror of my soul. In a Wonder Weaving thou has shown me my face as it is seen in thy mind. This magic mirror doth reflect my mind. Thou seeest thyself as my mind doth see. And what is more truthful than a mirror?"*

*"Ah,"*Ali said reassuringly, *"The Moon Girl hath a magic mirror. That mirror is her eyes."*

Her eyelids closed. She let fall the mirror to the sand. Then she touched his arm. *"Come stroll with me along this jeweled beach and mark how the sands do awake and sing when touched by the tide of the ocean's love. Dost thou see that glow of mauve far down the beach and moving upwards in the sky? That is the glow of the burning vessel that brought thee to my shore. There is now no ship to bear thee hence. But when one hath love that is strong as death what need hath he to wander more?"*

With no speech Ali contemplated the violet light of the distant shore.

Commented Gloriande, *"Thy silence speaketh assent."* Then she turned their footsteps towards the forest trees.

"Now art thou freed from all earth and care of worldly things. And now thou shalt behold the Moon Girl. She cometh to one in dreams. Already the night is far advanced. I have prepared for thee a place where thine eyes must slumber and sleep while thy soul doth rejoice in dreamland. Give thyself to my guidance."

With soundless footsteps they trod a pathway moss-carpeted through a bosky grove dim-lighted by huge glow-worms on grassy mounds. They halted at a little alabaster chapel half-hidden by black cypress trees. Her hands then played upon a latchet until it yielded and a door opened silent as an eyelid. She entered and lit a little taper which revealed a sumptuous room carpeted and tapestried and embellished with strange swords and symbols. Here hung Turkish scimitars and carvings in wood and stone. Here were statuettes on pedestals and chief among them was a marble statue of a goddess nude and blind. The domed ceiling was of a dark blue spangled with little stars of silver and from this little dome, on golden chain, hung a lamp of beryl curved like the horned crescent of the star of Aphrodite. This lamp she lighted. It shone with a palpitating fire and it breathed forth an enthralling incense. She drew aside a curtain and revealed a couch upon which she relaxed in restful attitude.

"On this couch doth thou sleep until the Moon Girl doth awaken thy soul."

Ali took a backward step.

She rose. *"What hast thou to fear? Thou art safe beyond telling. None but I know the pathway hither. Here, secure in this sacred chapel thou shalt pass the night alone. I shall return in the cool hour before the*

Morning Star; I shall awaken thy slumber and I shall ask if thou hast visioned the Moon Girl."

She pushed aside a secret marble panel in the wall and disclosed an alcove stored with alabaster vials. She plucked forth a casolette whose perfume captured all the room. She placed it on a tabouret beside the couch and lifted the casket lid. Forth came a fragrance of such potency that would divest a strong man of all will.

"This is the supreme of all earth's odors. This is the essence of the Perfume of Dreams. Sleep now, brave Prince Ali, and in dreams thou shalt experience Paradise and meet the Moon Girl there. Sleep now, brave heart. Sweet be thy rest after danger-days in loveless lands. Sleep."

Her soft hand soothed his brow. His eyelids closed. She withdrew, silent as a shadow, and left the agate lamp still burning overhead. She hastened to her palace.

Ali felt his shoulders rudely shaken. *"Wake up! Wake up! Fool of fools! Dream-drunk in the lap of danger. Haste thee! Rouse thy bones!"*

It was Agha Pha who pulled the dreamer from his couch. Scarce could Ali speak. Agha quickly smothered the casolette in a dried fish skin and tucked it within his tunic.

"Strange that this perfume in its concentration hath not killed thee stark outright. This essence is the most overpowering in the world. It is the odor of Isis. It shall be my ransom for rescuing thee. Now put wings to thy feet."

"What meaneth all this molestation?"

"I shall tell thee later. Mouzaac and I have sought thee all this night. We mistrusted the meaning of that

white dove home-flying. At thy departure we did suspicion a motive, and we sat forth to rescue. Already Mouzaac hath despaired the search. But, mounting a little donkey, I searched the sandy shore. Detecting this odor coming from the forest I followed the clue unto this alabaster tomb. And here I find Ali, the Fool, dream-drowned and senseless. Awake dodder-head! The empress of Fools hath thee in thrall. Fly with me now, right now!"

"I must await the word of Gloriande. She must be obeyed. The glorious, glamorous, golden Gloriande. She returneth anon."

"Ah, ha, ha, ha! Thy snout is still smeared with the drug of the Queen of Sirens. Yes. She will come; but she will leave thee dead in this, thy tomb. All around us are little sepulchers and grassy mounds that cover the mould of heroes who, for a little while, were lovers of thy Enchantress. Thinkest thou that she, the great queen of the Moon's isle, shall permit any swain to strut the world boasting, even to himself how he hath found favors of the queen? Haste thee! Dodder-head! The morning star of a new day is at hand."

Ali sat as in a trance. *"Some strange thing dropped there on the door-sill. What made that moving shadow in the doorway?"* he muttered.

"It was only the beast that bore me hither. He is impatient of delay. Haste thee! He shall take us both together on his back."

They gained the doorway. With a gasp exclaimed Agha Pha, *"Behold! The ass is dead! This concentrated odor hath killed the beast outright. Obey me, Ali. Assist me lift this carcass."*

They dragged the dead ass to the couch, pillowed his head and overspread him with splendid coverlets. *"Now let the Siren find another ass than the one she pillowed on these cushions."*

Then Agha Pha leaped upon the couch and unhooked the lamp of beryl. He splashed its essence upon the dead, dumb beast and took with him the lamp. Ali and Agha escaped into the cool hour before the dawn.

To their ears came the sound of riotous revelry in the palace grounds - a trumpeting and a drumming and a beating of brazen gongs.

Said Agha Pha, *"You hear the climax of what they know here as the Carnival of Blood. While this uproar raves thus in the Palace grounds a band of swordsmen, before the eyes of the throng, are slaying a gang of pirates bolt upright who were enticed to this carnival unheeding the fate that awaits them. The pirate ship is even now laden with loot from this island and elsewhere – laden with precious stones and metals and with perfumes and spiceries and gossamer weavings of thinnest texture. That ship now rocks in the harbor awaiting the morning tide which at this season of the year ebbs outward to safety on the great sea ocean. Haste thee, Ali! Mouzaac and his men and all thy troubadours and musicians have taken over and manned that ship and as soon as we arrive they will sail."*

"The moon looks on many brooks
But the broooks adore one moon."

— Unknown

"There was a mirror inside me which colored all it reflected There was a lute or a harp that sang as the wind sings"

— Unknown

Chapter Seven

Bélhamarámara!

here were days and there were nights, and ever the treasure-laden barge was blown by friendly winds through windows of wandering foam on dark blue seas. The watchful eye of Mouzaac caught never a sail of any kind, caught never a green isle, and never a bird. Some of the crew began to fear they might never see land again.

Then came a night, when in the hour of deepest dark Mouzaac on the look-out exclaimed, *"The port! The Port of Eutukia! That glimmer on the edge of the sky is the gleam of the great phare which burns on the topmost terrace of the Temple of Fortune."*

When the morn morrowed they looked upon a goodly shore long and level and with peaks of mountains far beyond.

Through a narrow entrance they sailed into the broad bowl of the harbor which was embraced by a far-flung city, grateful to the eye. In the center of this city rose a table-land of rose-hued stone, an acropolis on whose summit was a fire kept burning night and day, a phare for the ships out on the ocean. This was the temple of the goddess Fortuna. It shone like burnished gold and silver and all the terraces were graced with trees and hanging verdure. At the base of the acropolis was a great gate through which only privileged personages could pass. On either side of this gate broad diverging highways extended across the shoreline out to the two verdant little islands in the bay.

On each of the little islands were graceful pavilions amid palm trees and gardens. Said Ali, *"How delightful to the eye are these two islands in the bay."*

Said Mouzaac, *"Yes, delightful to the eye. That island to the left is the delight of gamesters and mountebanks and fortune tellers and dealers in doubtful monies. Observe in the center of the isle an alabaster building with the cubic towers. Some call that the Pavilion of Fate. In that pavilion is preserved a set of ancient dice which some claim are the very dice that were cast for the Master's cloak. From all quarters of the world come people to that pavilion in search of the fortune tellers who can give them glimpses into their fates. The gamesters purchase lucky amulets and lucky birthday stones and disport themselves in games of dice and wheels of fortune and in other play things of the gamblers. In one of these games the players delight in casting noisy dice large as coconuts. Some of the gamesters enjoy themselves there but a day and slay themselves before the night morrows."*

"And what are the virtues of the Isle on the right?"

"A blameless place because it is ward of industry. In that isle are all sorts of handicraft that please the eye. There are cutters of stone and carvers of silver and gold and blenders of perfumes and eye powders and face powders and pencils for eyebrows and eyelids. But chief of all the workers there is in the great Hall of Weavers. It is the largest building. You see it in the center of them all. In there are woven robes for every royal monarch and tapestries for opulent dining halls and throne rooms and for sacred shrines. These workers seek to guard the secret of this weaving."

"Is the Holy Garment enshrined in that hall?" asked Ali.

"Nay, not there. It is enshrined somewhere in yonder distant chain of mountains which are the boundary of the little realm of Eutukia, and few indeed are they who know the sacred hiding place."

Midway between the two diverging causeways stood the Casino, a great cubic hall where a festival of merchandise was always on display. Here were bazaars of extraordinary weavings and of dyes of Tryrian purple and of vermillion of the orient. Here were ivories and workings in mahogany and teak and sundry dried fruits and spiceries and rare minerals like quicksilver and orpiment red and yellow and Arabian ointments.

Here Mouzaac moored his barque. Straightway he exchanged his shop for a caravan of camels, dromedaries, pack mules and donkeys. He removed from the ship chests of treasures for he had been told that his store of royal worth was a magic key to open the bronze doors of the Acropolis.

There was a grand arena where charioteers and bull fighters and gladiators brought resounding applause from gay crowds. There were also halls of music and studios of sculpture and painting and extensive libraries. But Ali passed by all these wonders and at the Hall of Weavers he enquired for the Mistress of the Weavers named Penelope.

Said a grim guardian at the portal, *"What errand is thine? And by what authority dost thou ask to interfere with the industries of this busy mart?"*

Answered Ali, *"I bring a message from Queen Fortunata's sister whose signet ring I wear."*

The guardsman scrutinized the signet ring and after further enquiries replied, *"Sit ye in yonder anteroom. Penelope shall hear thee."*

In came a woman tall in stature, straight and spare, silver haired and with long claw-like fingers. The emaciation of her face enlarged her jet black fearsome eyes which rolled with a hungry haunted searching stare. She bore a staff.

"What man art thou? And wherefore here?"

"Miriam of the Thorns hath directed me hither."

"Make brief thy say for I am permitted but small respite from my daily task. Is this some subterfuge, some trickery on thy part to harass my all too unhappy soul? How am I to know that thou comest from honest Miriam?"

"By this signet ring," replied Ali.

Transfigured she stood and leaned upon her staff. Eagerly she cross-questioned Ali and from him brought out the stories of his adventure.

When he spoke of the shrine of the garment she exclaimed in piercing tones, *"I alone in Eutukia can lead thee to the Robe. Even our Sultana knoweth not the way. The shrine lieth on the outer boundaries of her realm. As to the Sibyl of Stone I know her well. I am of the sisterhood of her Grotto."*

She gave way to sudden weeping, and leaning on her staff, exclaimed, *"Star-guided mariner be thou my deliverer! I will guide thee to the Shrine of the Robe and to the Sibyl of Stone."*

Much did Ali marvel at her tense emotions which moved his own eyes to tears and he implored that she confide somewhat of her life.

"I am perforce a vassal to our Sultana for lo these many years. In penance they made me mistress of the weavers here. They gave to me the name Penelope but my real name of Mariandyni! By right I am of the noble Sisterhood of the Sibyl of Stone. By a cruel injustice I have been here a slave. Thou art he who can deliver me."

"Worthy Mariandyni! I am at thy service. How may I rescue thee from thy thralldom in Eutukia?"

"I know well the whims of our empress Fortunata. She is prone to fickleness. That signet ring may win thee audience, but if thy story doth not beguile her she might consign thee to the gladiatorial ring as a diversion among the bloody games. Thou hast gained the graces of capricious Gloriande of the Island of the Moon by a woven likeness of her face; do then likewise for Fortunata the Fickle. If by that thou winnest favor ask that thou be granted to see the Shrine of the Garment. In that moment I shall declare myself as worthy to lead the way for thee and thy caravan not only to the Shrine but also to the Oracle of Stone which lieth far beyond. But I advise thee to withhold the ring her from sight until thou hast made sure what the whimsies of her mind may be."

Came the day when Ali, with all his retinue and caravan, saluted the closed gate of the acropolis and sought entrance there. The guardian of the gate heard Ali to the end. Then said he, *"Thy quest is to be commended and thy comrades are of noble bearing and thou hast treasures worthy of royal desires. But already a full quota of visitors hath passed these gateways through today and it is not auspicious to overburden our Sultana with a surfeit of complaint and pleading. Some other day for thee."*

"Worthy guardsman faithful in thy office. I am bearing to the Sultana something that will outweigh all wealth. I bear a ring a token from the Sultana's sister Bonnechance. This must be presented by myself to the Sultana of Eutukia."

The guardian feasted his eyes with this treasured trinket while Ali related how it had been wished upon him. Straightway the keeper commanded, *"Let the gates open."*

Then to the appointed messenger he said, *"Advise the Sultana that cometh here a goodly worthy man on urgent mission and who can recount a stirring, thrilling history and a rare story which is unaccustomed to her ear. Advise her highness that it doth augur well that she give this man the first hearing although he is the last one among the many pilgrims and emissaries who already are in this enclosure waiting her audience."*

The cavalcade of laden camels and dromedaries and mules filed into the inner citadel. There they tarried waiting until a messenger from Fortunata announced she was prepared to meet the many men who had journeyed from the world's four quarters to speak their errands before her throne. The queen's messenger escorted the pilgrims into the Chamber and assigned their places of waiting. Ali was to be the first to state his quest.

He found himself in a hall of sumptuous invention, a flamboyancy of ivory and gold and jade and of draperies of Tyrian dye and of hangings of cloth-of-gold embell-ished with symbols done in jetty black. A heavy carpet covered all the floor. Overhead a trellis supported a grapevine of fine gold from which depended clusters of grapes in divers hues: some green, some yellow, some rosy and some purple, and every grape a gem-stone in its natural lustre. There were cushioned seats of jasper and crystal. And there were little tabourets of amethyst and topaz. At the end of the chamber, on a dais which extended clear across the hall, was a chryselephantine throne-chair of gold and ivory. And directly behind this chair was a discus of gold fashioned like a wheel whose many spokes pierced the ferrule in tapering tips. To the right and the left of this chair groups of negritio guards-men took their station with scimitars of polished steel. Then from a wing of the dais came a procession of slave girls with hair black and bushy and eyes like those of Egyptian portraits. They were beating tambourines and tabors, and each one was more lovely than the one who came before her. The procession filled the length of the entire dias. There they stood a moment in their loveliness and at a signal all sat down upon the floor.

Last of all, to the lilt of lute and the throb of cithera, appeared the Sultana, a glorious face and figure with hair of a blend of gold and bronze and eyes of bright greenish blue that shone with a restless discontent. She sat in the throne chair and her face was in the center of the discus just behind. Immediately the resplendent wheel of Fortunata began slowly to revolve.

A negroid guardsman placed Ali directly in front of the Sultana.

"Who standeth before me? Whence come? And whither bound? Why demandeth my attention?"

"I am Ali, a weaver of dream faces bound for the Well at the World's End. I sojourn in Eutukia that I may learn the secret of the craft of the most surpassing weaving in the world. For that secret of great weaving I would give an ample share of treasures."

"Wandering weaver, I have a surfeit of worldly things. I reap where I have never sown; I gather where I have never toiled . To those who catch my fancy I sometimes toss a guerdon. From him who doth cloy my eyes and ears I take even that which he hath - even his own life. What hath thou to catch my fancy? Today I am irked and angered."

She seemed in a frame of fretful humor. At once rose murmurings of wondering in the assembly.

"O Princess, exalted, adored and feared, whose favors are sought by Sultan and by slave and whose wealth is fabulous beyond compute I blush to recount what I can offer for I behold this palace full-garnished with rare gems well-set in silver and gold and ivory, and hung with tapestries of surpassing merit. But I am come with a treasure ship heavy with rare metals and

precious stones and with enthralling perfumes and delectable preserves and fruits for royal boards, and divers rarities rich and strange. Of these treasures choose thy choice if thou wilt instruct me in the world's most wondrous weaving."

"To me all the cleverness of the goldsmiths and of lapidaries are but as toys of tin because of their abundance in my halls. What art hast thou to beguile me, to hold me in thrall for a moment, for the tedium of life is ever at my heels."

"O Queen, the art of music doth for the moment rescue the soul from every cark and care. I have here with me a band of troubadours whose sweet words and voices can rescue thy soul from cark and care, can transport thee into realms of rapture by relating of their wild adventures."

"The telling of past days are of idle event to me. I am not concerned with yesterday nor with tomorrow. My ears are grown quite cloyed with the music of the world. Give me something devoid of sound. Some show in silence."

"Ah. Princess, I have here also my Pantomime players, lithesome acrobats, who can act out a silent show with all the charm of song and music, but act it out to secret silent harmonies. Only by rhythmic movements can this band of voiceless men express the ardent life within them."

"They would be but childish marionettes to me. The tedium of life bites my heel. But what canst thou of thyself express to me - what clever caper – what prestidigitation or pleasance canst thou conjure for my eye?"

"I am Ali the weaver of dream faces. Command thy worthy Mistress of Weavers, Penelope, to place before me here a loom and in a trice I will portray thee dream-faced as never before."

Lightly she laughed. *"Now thou dost catch my fugitive attention. A dainty boast is thine, O weaver, My palace is cloyed with weavings of rare device. I challenge thee to equal them. O journeyman weaver, make good thy words. Deign not to deceive my expectation. I ween this may be some clever foolery on thy part but surely it doth befool me for the moment. So on with this trickery."*

"Request thy Penelope to supply me only with a loom and I shall prove me."

To a group of attending women she called out, *"Is my Penelope among your group? Yes? Fetch the best loom for a weaving."*

While Penelope was fetching and preparing the loom before Fortunata, Ali stood before the queen in silence. His eyes burning with an unnatural fire as into the eyes of the Sultana he gazed. She felt a fascination in his stare. Ali closed his eyelids and with upturned face like one in a trance he said then in the language of the grasshoppers, *"O Soul of Lucifer, Soul of the shining stars! Puissant Gabalouk!* ***Bélhamarámara!*** *Hear my heart! O thou Patron of the gossamer weavers, who wind-wafted by thy will, trust thy guidance. Hear my heart! I trust thy guidance. Terrify my fingers into a wizardry of weaving! Aid me now or never! Hear the heart of thy child, O Gabalouk."*

A wind blew into the hall and rustled all the tapestries on the walls and agitated all the bird cages from which came cries of ravens and macaws and parrots. He wrapped his eyes with a scarf. Then Ali fell into a trance in which his soul found itself in Dreamland. There he saw the Ideal of Fortunata's face. Ali put his fingers to the task. He drew his magic bobbins from his belt. To and fro the nimble shuttle leaped as though shot by lightning. From his enchanted bobbins Ali drew his ever ample threads, and in so brief a time was the work done that Fortunata was wonder-eyed at her likeness, dream-featured and with radiant hair of reddish gold and with a pale green symbol of the Moon Girl just above her brow. The woven, silken threads began to pulsate with living light as tiny flashes of enlivenments danced within the weaving and formed the sacred words:

Then the entire weaving became a luminous radiance of supernal beauty - a living portrait of a divine soul breathing forth the loving fragrance of the Magna Mater.

Long she looked upon this silken threaded prodigy.

"This is what I was born to be but am not. Thous hast made a miracle before my eyes. It doth consume me. It doth exalt me. It doth enthrall me."

A silence of expectation held throughout the hall. Then Penelope rushed to the front, and holding the weaving up to view, proclaimed, *"Man hath not woven this; only madness could have done it!"*

When the universal applause subsided, Fortunata addressed Ali, *"Thou wizard of weaving! Name thy recompense."*

"Gracious Sultana! Give me leave to look upon the weaving in the Robe which is guarded in a shrine in thy land."

"Thou hast named the very last favor I would grant, and thou art the first to make this asking. Who hath told thee of the Shrine of the Garment?"

"One of thy sisters, Lady Miriam of the Crown of Thorns."

"By what token may I grant credence to that tale?"

"By the token of this ring. La Belle Dame Bonnechance hath placed it upon my finger, a signet ring from thy sister."

"A signet ring from Bonnechance! My sisters wander willy-nilly in the highways of the world and dispense capricious chances good or ill. Often time they mask themselves with age or ugliness, but all of my sisters are really lovely as the Moon. But thou hast over-asked. The keeper of the Sanctuary may not obey my order. One must recount to her the saying that sings. I know not the saying.

"Furthermore, I know of no guide to point the way for thee."

Straightway strode forth Penelope gowned in a robe of deep purple, the color of which made her melancholy face more pallid. She paused, bowed head before the Sultana while she said, *"Most exalted Fortunata, I know well the Saying that Sings. I know the path to that shrine. Is there aught of weaving that I do not know? I know the woman who is keeper of the Garment. Grant that I may lead the worthy weaver thither."*

"My faithful Penelope! Thou hast been dutiful in years of service. I grant here and now the reward of freedom. Guide this weaver to the Robe. At the end of thy journey thou art free."

Penelope prostrated her form at the feet of Fortunata while the handmaidens chanted the ritual of freeing a woman of bondage to the queen.

She rose, and facing the assembly proclaimed, *"Henceforth I am Mariandyni."*

When Ali and his comrades had withdrawn from the Palace of Fortunata with Mariandyni, debated they concerning the journey to the Shrine. Said Ali to Mariandymi, *"Is the Holy Garment enshrined in a wall known to the wise men as the Stone of Silence?"*

"Not so, Prince Ali, not so. That stone is treasured in the grotto of the great sibyl who is known as the Sibyl of Stone. I will lead thee later to that grotto."

Then Agha Pha enquired, *"They say the perfume of the Sibyl of Stone prevaileth over the odors of all other sibyls or sultanas or witches. May I hope to know that perfume?"*

"It is a perfume richer than the Rose of Kashmir. It is not to be sought. It will seek thee."

"Name the reward for thy guidance," commanded Ali.

"My reward for all service shall be these: I must ride on a white camel caparisoned with little bells of gold. I must have a body guard of black swordsmen and a band of musicians and trumpeters."

Chapter Eight

The Stone of Silence

ame the day when out of the city of Eutukia marched a caravan royally arrayed with trappings and banners and gonfalons and pennants and led by a silver-haired woman high-placed and canopied on a milk white camel tinkling with golden bells. Following the camel came a troop of black guardsmen on white horses. Then came a train of camels, dromedaries and donkeys.

Over the realm of Eutukia they rode. A goodly land it was and grateful to the eye. On the green savannas were occasional groves of trees laden with kindly fruits. Some bore a meal that could be made into a bread of good savor and some bore good honey; and there were trees whose sap was a very good wine. It was a land where men need not contend with a niggardly soil for sustenance. It was a land which invited a leisure beside lazy streams which serpentined between low banks of green sod.

They proceeded directly across the land of Eutukia to the Wall of Mountains which were the high boundary between the Land of Sacred Stone. For many a league they skirted the base of this wall and passed by the dwellings of sheiks and shepherds and vintners and makers of cheese and merchants of excellent honies and fruits of the date palms and fig trees. Farther on they passed tent makers and tailors and weavers of holy rugs and carvers of holy images, amulets and beads for rosaries. They came at last to the Honey Comb Rocks where the sheer mountainside bore rock cut temples and shrines large and small and where dwelled holy hermits and also brutish troglodytes, who were dwarfish and hairy of body and limb. Here they turned into a cleft in the Wall of Mountains where the rock wall had been split asunder by some convulsion of the earth in some remote eon of time. A savage chasm it was and fearful to the eye. This was the Via Media, the Middle Way of the World (the boundary between Eutukia and the Land of Stones.) Between these lofty ruin rocks Mariandyni directed the caravan to proceed. In these walls were caves which growled with muffled thunders and caves which belched forth sulphurous fumes. The springs in this cleft were salty as tears and bitter as remorse. At times the tremblings of the earth rolled down huge round stones with awful crashings. Just inside this chasm was a lodge that housed a certain small bazaar sequestered in a wrinkle of the stony wall. It was surrounded with a garden which extended to the wall of the cliff. This bazaar was a fragrant dell of rugs and tapestries lighted by a chain-hung lamp and tended by a patriarchal man, white bearded, spectacled and wearing a silk turban over his baldness. This cell was like a sacristy. Here were prayer rugs and sacerdotal vestments and sacred censers and utensils, and altar cloths of dyes incarnadine. Here were ointments and fragrant gums and spices and frankincense and myrrh.

Here were ancient manuscripts of the lost books of Holy Scripture.

Here halted the caravan while Mariandyni led Ali and Ferista within. They found the Patriarch absorbed in a scroll of rabbinical wisdom. He placed his finger on where he was reading, and, looking over his spectacles, he enquired, *"What can I do for you?"*

"Worthy custodian of the Sacred Relic give us a guide to the upper Chamber."

Rising with kindly smile the Patriarch answered, *"Where is any Upper Chamber here?"*

Pointing upwards, Mariandyni answered, *"Well do I know the Shrine of the Robe, the Upper Chamber high above us. I am deputed by Fortunata, the queen of this thy land, to guide here a worthy weaver who hath enchanted Fortunata with a most miraculous weaving and to ask that he be allowed to see the Robe."*

The Patriarch removed his glasses. *"An edict of Fortunata is no coin of prevalence in this shrine. We are not beholden to any queen or monarch of the world. We are our own authority here."*

"I am come on my own authority. I am Mariandyni of the Sisterhood of the Sibyl of Stone, long exiled in the city of Fortuna, where under the name of Penelope I presided over every weaving there. Therefore I am a born inheritrix of the right to look upon the Robe."

"I do recall thee now. Thou hast been here before. But how changed is all thine aspect now! Sunsets thou hast suffered as many a Mary hath done. But this man? By what credentials cometh he here?"

"By the insignia of Miriam of the Crown of Thorns. He beareth her signet ring and magic belt she gave him which is fashioned to bear a portion of the perfume of the Robe - the Perfume of Great Price."

During this colloquy a tall dark-eyed woman was slowly stepping forward from the depths of the bazaar.

She interjected, *"I, too, am a Mary. I have heard this disputation from my place behind the curtain."*

To the Patriarch she said, *"The words of this woman findeth favor with me. Well do I know this Mariandyni. Her mother was Mariani, child of Mariammitani, who was born of Mareotis, a child of Marea who was born of the house of Mariamne. She is descended of the line of the great Maria who designed the Robe of the Master."*

Then she bowed her head and spoke, *"I, too, am a Mary. I, too, have suffered as many a Mary."*

The Patriarch, much moved by this speech answered, *"Most worthy Maria. I leave this woman and this man in thy charge."*

Promptly she led the men out into the garden behind the bazaar where a great round stone lay against the wall of the mountain. Then in a loud voice she called, *"Who will roll away the Stone?"*

At her command two swarthy dwarfish strong-shouldered troglodytes came up from below the bazaar and they rolled away the stone. To these she commanded, *"Guide these men to the Upper Chamber."*

The troglodytes lighted two lanterns. With Mariandyni leading, Ali and his companions and their caravan followed the dim lights of their guides.

Emerging out of this long alley of the Middle Way of the World, the caravan issued into a grateful land. Here Mariandyni directed the way across an open plain to the banks of the River of Healing, whose distant source was in the Grotto of the Sibyl of Stone, and whose waters were said to be for the healing of nations. Along this river wound a trail followed by pilgrims bound for the Grotto in hopes of being healed. Some were trudging on foot, silent and solitary, and some were in troops traveling with camels and mules.

This trail led the caravan of Ali into a bosage, dense and darkened, overarched with interlacing branches of lofty trees like unto the mighty yew, the dense cypress and the regal holm oak from whose branches dangled long grey mosses. It seemed like unto a region of haunted shade, a Grove of Styx.

The precincts of the Sibyl abounded in shrines and altars sacred to unknown gods and to divers spirits of healing.

On a bypath through this gloomsome grove filed silent white-faced women robed in black, marching in measured steps to the entrance of an alabaster shrine, where they halted to chant a mournful and monotonous litany. Farther on stood an altar in front of a strange carving in stone.

At the end of the trail the caravan marched full into sunlight. They found themselves on the lofty rim of a vast and verdant amphitheater. In the midst thereof glistened a turquoise lake and from the center of this lake towered the Oracle of Stone. This treeless island on the lake was encircled by a wall with two gates: one to the rising sun and one to the west and from these gates causeways crossed the lake to the graveled beaches where groups of pilgrims bathed their ailing bodies.

A forest bordered all the beaches round the lake and amid trees were hostelries, caravanseries, yards for cattle, and little bazaars where merchants sold sacred images and lucky stones and phallic symbols and animals for sacrifice on the many altars in the region.

Of the multitudes of people who frequented these surroundings only a privileged few were permitted to enter the central Oracle of Stone where dwelled the renowned Sibyl.

This oracle was a hollow cone-shaped mass formed in bygone ages by some great upsprouting of molten magmas which had hardened into a pinnacled pile of vitreous rock of feldspar and olivine and magnetic ores. Jets of white vapors issued from scattered orifices in the stone and maintained a cap of cloud around its brow. From the yawning mouth of the grotto foamed a cascade which was the source of the River of Healing. An awesome, fearsome sight, it was replete with wildest prodigies of nature.

The caravan followed Mariandyni along the strip of bathing beaches to the causeway which led to the Sunrise Gate of the Shrine. Here they halted for the night. Out of the groves came hostlers who led the beasts of burden to their proper enclosures and pages who conducted the people to appropriate hostelries.

As soon as morning morrowed Mariandyni, high perched on her camel, led the way across the board causeway to the Sunrise Gate. Ali and his comrades and his blind musicians and dumb acrobats followed on foot. In a watch tower above the gate sat a grizzled old man in helmet and breast plate watching the approaching procession and when Mariandyni saluted this tower the churlish keeper called, *"What mob is this that cometh here at unseemly hour commanded by an old woman?*

"I am not the captain," responded Mariandyni. *"I am but the guide; I bid the captain answer thee."*

Ali strode forward to announce, *"I am Ali of Ingdad bent on friendly mission to the Oracle of the Land of Stone to know the litany of the Stone of Silence. I have with me offerings of precious stones and rare balsams and pollen and silver and gold."*

Replied the keeper, *"Think not to win our Sibyl's favor with worldly goods. A worthy purpose doth move her more than bribes of silver and gold. She hath great store of precious stones and metals. But who are all these blind men with you?"*

"They live to make music and of such sweetness that can melt a heart of stone into tears of joy."

"Our Sibyl hath small need of music. The walls of her chamber sing new songs to her by day and by night. And who are all these silent fellows standing back of the blind men?"

"They can answer thee only in action for their ears and their throats are as stones. But all these deaf and dumb men are actors in a telling pantomime."

"She hath no need of freakish fellows leading a band of blind men to the whims of an old woman."

He made as though to close the shutter but the woman's voice rang out, *"I demand an open door! Well do I know thee, impious Krutar! I am Mariandyni, long in exile from this oracle, penalized to remain away until able to lead hither high-minded men. I have paid my penalty! I have found the men. Here they stand far more worthy of this shrine than thyself. I have served my sentence. Let us in!"*

"Hateful hag! Thou are not Mariandyni. She was young and beautiful and soft of speech. Sheath the dagger of thy tongue and go."

"Had not my tongue been the Stone of Silence thou, and not I, would have been banished from this Shrine. Thy falsified accusation banished me. If thou wouldst keep my tongue a stone of silence let me in!"

Then she uttered mystic words which Ali did not understand, and which paled the face of Krutar. Straightaway the twin doors opened on sounding hinges and all the envoys entered in.

Then Mariandyni led the way to a smaller gate in an inner wall of blocks of topaz and basalt. This gate was garnished with mother-of-pearl. Just above this pearly gate an oriel window jutted from the wall. Three times did Mariandyni halloo but no response from the window came. At this she stood up in the litter and with her staff she smote the latticed window panes.

The window flew open and disclosed the face of a fair maid. Surprised, she said, *"Who art thou, O crazy crone. Who let thee through the outer gate? None hath appraised me of thy coming."*

"I am come to take back my lost office of Keeper of this Gate of Pearl."

"Mad old hag! Thou dost affright me! What manner of men are with thee? The Sibyl's guards shall seize ye all!"

With that she made a shrilling call for aid. Promptly the gate was opened and out came a troop of grey-bearded guardsmen with swords and halbreds and they conducted all the party to the Pavilion of the Seneschal for a hearing.

The Seneschal was a gracious man of kindly speech and with long grey beard and snow white hair and quiet eyes of blue. The strange woman stood before him and spoke, *"Dost thou not remember Mariandyni?"*

"O sister Mariandyni! How changed in aspect is thy face that once was as the morning to look upon. Why art thou here and who are they that come with thee?"

"I am come to announce the finish of my penance and reclaim my rightful office as Keeper of the Pearl Gate. Behold! I come canopied on a white camel garlanded with little golden bells just as I was penalized to do, and I bring with me men wise and with a wondrous tale to tell just as our Sibyl commanded it should be."

After he reviewed the strange case of Mariandyni the Seneschal gave ear to Ali who responded, *"I am Ali, the Weaver of Ingdad, the Eye of the Desert, hither come to know the secrets of the Stones that Sing and the Stones that See and of the Stone of Silence."*

Then briefly he recounted his adventures and concluded, *"I have with me a chorus of singers sweet as sleep and a band of acrobats who without words enthrall the eye with mystery play."*

"Of a truth thou bearest the perfume of adventure and our Sibyl is pleased with magic words when sung to instrumental sounds; and there are certain divine truths which can be best expressed with mystic pantomime."

"Now this man is Mariner Mouzaac who knoweth well the circle of the world and the manners and customs of men. He desireth to know all the wonder places ere he die. He hath braved all the waves of the wide sea-ocean and prevailed over all sea furors. He hath toiled beyond the strength and the days of a brave old age and hath hither come in his last days to revive his strength in the River of Healing."

"Our Sibyl loveth the well-seasoned tales of hardy mariners. Methinks she may grant strength to this worthy wanderer."

"And this man, Agha Pha, is the Prince of the Land of Perfumes who bringeth a harmony of odors and savors and incense which he hath collected from all the fragrant places in the world. Through these perfumes he is gifted to create any mood or emotion in the mind or in the soul, be that mood sensuous or holy or of divine melancholy or divine ecstasy."

"Our Sibyl hath experienced every attar, every essence and every distillation which delight mankind. She hath here a perfume that overpowerth all others in the world, a perfume potent to melt a stormy heart to tears, a perfume to ennoble the whole life of a man. But if this Prince of Perfume can express with his different odors all the moods that sway mankind he may persuade the Sibyl to reward him with a casket of the perfume for a heart of stone."

"I perceive that Mariandyni hath indeed brought hither three men of wisdom. She can be restored to office if these men hath tales of wonder that are true."

Ali continued, *"And lastly here is my boon companion, my fag, fear-haunted but faithful, who hath been at my side through dire dangers. His is a friend who faileth never. He hath in his soul a music which he hath never sung. In his thinkings he hath a perfume that riseth from trampled hopes. But he hath a heart too timid to relate them; therefore he hath no tale to tell."*

"Perhaps our Sibyl could awake his soul to song and his heart to courage. He hath a pleasant face and winsome. It is the trodden violet that giveth sweetest perfume. The Sibyl might welcome the perfume of his words."

When all had their say the Seneschal responded, *"Sister Mariandyni, thou hast brought hither three men well worthy of a hearing. I shall report to our Sibyl all that ye have told me. If perchance it pleaseth her she will grant each and all a hearing. But we must abide her bidding to appear."*

All the men were led to certain lodges to await the summons to the Court of the Sibyl. A woman conducted Mariandyni to another place meanwhile.

Came the appointed day when the Sibyl would hear the plaint of Mariandyni and her band. At hour of dawn the Seneschal conducted Ali to the Grotto of the Sibyl of the Stone before the Sibyl and attendants arrived.

It was a vast hollowness with a wide mouth that opened towards the dawn. Glooming daylight filtered through translucent vitreous walls. At the far side of the cavern was a cavity in the wall which revealed the inner side of a great flue up which rose subterranean vapors to a vent in the upper rock. In front of the cavity was the Throne of the Sibyl, a great black stone of magnetic ore which had fallen from the sky and over which lay leopard skins. In front of this cushioned stone a wide promenade extended across the cave and in front of this promenade was a moat of running water as black as the River Styx. Facing this throne and moat Ali and the Seneschal were the only people in the grotto. From the vaulted ceiling hung inverted pinnacles of vitreous rock studded with half molten jewels of divers hue.

Ali stood in wonderment awhile. Then to the Seneschal he said, *"Whence cometh this sweet low music all around us? It is as though these walls of glassy stone of themselves are crooning harmonies."*

"Rightly hast thou imagined. These walls sing back a memory of old songs and music of all the tones which in this enclosure have been uttered. These walls drink in only harmonies and exhale them just as a great rock in a rainless land giveth back the warmth of the desert in the cool of a night. Likewise do these enchanted grotto walls sing, during the hours of quietude, the harmonies they hear above the tumult of the day."

From the right of the throne marched in a silent procession of maidens with faces like rose buds and figures enrobed in heliotrope spangled with gold. Upon their shoulders fell locks of golden hair. Two of these maidens escorted Mariandyni still wearing her ragged sackcloth gown. The black waters of the moat reflected inverted images of these marchers.

From the left side of the oracle came a procession of men with hoary hair and long grey beards and with them was the aged mariner Mouzaac. Then forth from a tunnel below the throne came a priestess leading a chorus of white robed temple girls bearing golden harps and cymbals. Straight way these girls broke into song and music to announce that the great SHE was about to appear.

From a place behind the throne in marched the Sibyl of Stone. Silence fell upon the grotto. The Sibyl was a resplendence in white. Her coal black hair was parted in the middle and drawn behind in long plaits and a black ribbon encircled her forehead. Her waist and wrists and arms and ankles were banded with pearls and from her girdle depended strands of pearls all around. She took seat upon the stone and her splendor reflected from the black water. The rays of the rising sun shining through the mouth of the grotto fell upon her face which was of a cold imperial beauty somewhat haughty.

In that moment the priestess repeated the Salutation to the Sunrise accompanied by the instrumental music of her maids.

Spoke the Sibyl, *"We are here assembled to consider Sister Mariandyni who, after long exile, doth plead to be restored to the Keepers of the oracle."*

Mariandyni walked forward and stood in waiting. *"Where are her accusers now?"*

Not one accuser appeared.

"Where are they who will plead the cause of Mariandyni?"

Promptly in marched Ali's musicians and pantomime men all garbed in white and crowned with laurel. Close in front of the throne they stood, while the Prince of Perfume came to join them with a group of young men bearing covered censers. Immediately the singers uttered pleading notes accompanied by appropriate gestures of the silent actors and while arias rose and fell in moods of hope and longing and penitence and contrition. Aga Pha released a perfume for each mood. This correspondence of tone and gesture and perfume moved the Sibyl of Stone to tear-bright eyes. Seeing this the Prince of Perfume signaled his pageant to notes of pardon and remission and then to joy and resounding thanksgiving.

The Sibyl closed her eyes and upturned her face. Her bosom heaved with panting. Her soul swelled with frenzy and her hair unwound from its braids.

Silence fell upon the entire assembly. Said the Sibyl, *"Bring forth the Stone of Silence."*

A woman in red brought forth from a receptacle in the wall one alabaster jar which glowed from some inward fire and which she placed at the feet of the Sibyl. She uncovered the jar to pluck forth a jet black stone and facing forward she held up the stone to view.

"What stone is this?" asked the Sibyl.

Answered the woman, *"This is the stone that would have been flung had not the words of the Master stayed the hand of the slinger. This is the penalty stone that was never flung after all the accusers grew dumb. This is the Stone of Silence."*

A portentous hush fell upon all in the chamber while each heart heard its own self accusations.

Spoke the Sibyl, *"Repeat the saying of the Stone of Silence."*

Replied the woman in red, *"Lift the stone and I am there."*

Promptly the choir of temple girls responded, *"Lift the stone of evil-mindedness from thy heart and thou shalt see God."*

Then one of the white-haired men stepped forth to return the Stone to its crypt in the stony wall.

It was indeed a miraculous stone which had fallen from the heavens - a hard and heavy stone of magnetic metals - a crystallized adamant which must have been forged in hell.

"Now let Sister Mariandyni be brought before me."

The young woman placed the aged one before the Sibyl of Stone.

"O Mariandyni, thy heart hath been purified by the fire of suffering. My heart hath been moved to compassion by the wise men thou hath guided hither. In the name of the great Magna Mater - the divine Mother of

Mercy – I grant thee the grace of pardon. Let Mariandyni be restored to all that she hath lost."

Then the woman tossed Mariandyni into the waters of healing. A plunge and splash and she sank below all seeing. When she reappeared she had the loveliness of youth. The maidens hastened to her as she emerged from the water and embraced her and robed her in a mantle of mauve such as the other sisters wore. Mariandyni took her place among her sisters who chanted a resurrection hymn.

Then to Agha Pha the Sibyl said, *"O Prince of Perfume, it is indeed of wonder that in this world of wide corruption so much fragrance prevaileth always over all. I shall grant thee the perfume of this Oracle."*

"Gracious Sibyl, since I have entered here, the perfume of the place hath lifted from my soul a stone."

"Thou shalt be granted a vial of this fragrance which is sacred to the great Mother Goddess. It is the most enduring of all perfumes. It is the perfume of a mother's love. I shall reward all the men that Mariandyni hath brought before me."

To the grey-bearded men she said, *"My Seneschal hath greatly moved me with the life of this old mariner. He is so worthy of great reward. Let what has been lost to Mouzaac in his world wanderings be restored to him."*

A grey-bearded priest led Mouzaac into the water, and lo, he came forth a young man in his prime.

Then towards Ali, who had sat in silence beside the Seneschal during all these prodigies, she cast her eyes and said, *"O Ali, most noble weaver, my Seneschal hath told me how and why thou made long pilgrimage to us here. May the gods of fortune lead thee to the Stones that Sing and the Stones that See. Thou hast already heard the mystery of the Stone of Silence."*

Then she made to him a long and commendatory

address which made all the people look upon Ali with wonder.

Then came the finale. Great shouts of joy and song and clash of cymbals and of smitten strings. The very walls responded with their mountainous throat. The instruments of Ali's band joined in of their own accord in uttering the great Hymn to the Mother of the Gods - to the Magna Mater. It was as though a tempest was playing upon vast organ pipes tuned to thunder.

When Ali and all his band made ready to depart from the oracle, the Seneschal sought him to announce, *"The Sibyl has arranged that thou must leave by the western gate and the keeper of that gate will supply thee with a guide that will lead by caravan even to the Well at the World's End."*

The causeways led across the lake with one gate kissed by the sunrise and other soothed by sunset. When the caravan of Ali attained to the Sunset Gate the Keeper saluted and said, *"Prince Ali, Our Lady, the exalted Sibyl, hath advised me of thy departure and she hath instructed that I present to thee from her sacred animals the one that is best endowed to guide thee through the pathless land."*

He conducted Ali and Ferista through a park where were confined rare and exotic animals both great and small. Here were unicorns and behemoths and griffins and white lions large as oxen. At a certain door the Keeper halted to say, *"Let this be the beast for thy journey."* He unbarred a stable door and out trotted a snow white wooly donkey with pink eyes.

"What jest is this?" demanded Ali. *"By his eyes I see this beast is blind."*

"He needeth no eye to see the way. He goeth by the inner eye which hath the vision of the All-seeing Eye."

Ali asked, *"Shall it be bruited abroad in Ingdad that I,*

astride a stone-blind ass, led an army astray, hunting the Well at the World's End?"

"This is no jest, most noble Prince. The Sibyl hath trusted that you trust her. She hath appointed this guide who shall lead thee to the Stones that Sing and the Stones that See and to the Well at the World's End of the Way."

With Tryphan, the white donkey, they returned to the gate where the Keeper said, *"This gateway looketh towards the Region of Stones, a land of far distances, unshadowed, untrodden, and where the trace of every trail or treachery flyeth away with the winds. An unfriendly land grudgeth grass and sproutage, but thou hast a guide who knoweth what wind-bitten pastures and pools are hidden there and who shall lead thee to the Stones that See and the Stones that Sing."*

Chapter Nine

The Stones that Sing

eagues of travel brought them into a treeless land of little rain where the dwellers were mostly shepherds who tended breeds of meager cattle strange and somewhat goat-like in appearance. The villages of these people were of stone houses some of which had blocks of masonry with noble carvings quarried from some ruined shrine long overthrown and forgotten. Even the stone walls of the cattle enclosures displayed an occasional noble block which once had graced the facade of a palace. In one of the villages were the stumps of some once-lordly columns of the portico of the shrine of some forgotten god.

One morning a squad of horsemen galloped forward to greet the caravan. They were all young men of handsome athletic build mounted on proud horses from Arabia. They saluted Ali astride his white and wooly Tryphan and declared, *"Hail to thee, brave chieftain of a worthy caravan! We are sent from the City of the Sun to greet thee and escort thee to our city. We are devotees of Apollo, god of the sun and god of music and god of beautiful minds and bodies. For thy coming we have prepared an Apollonian festival of games and musical contests. We have been informed of thy coming and of thy quest for the noble inspirations of human life. We have heard of the wise men with thee and of thine inspired musicians. Gladly we shall welcome thee for we are of the ancient cult that doth prize perfect human bodies with divine minds attuned to lofty music - fitting temples for the Spirit of God that dwelleth in us all. Our City is all expectant of thy coming and our Priestly Chief awaiteth thee with welcome."*

They came into the City of the Sun at the hour when the Eye of Day was closing and when the household hearths of the humble homes were sending upwards streams of thin blue smoke like thank-offerings for the peaceful evening meal. They passed the fallen columns of a lordly temple and the ruined walls of sculptured palaces which once had housed priests and potentates of high degree.

The youthful horsemen of Apollo led the caravan into the agora of the city where was assembled a throng of townsmen. In a glad voice the Herald of the horsemen proclaimed the advent of the hero of Ingdad, the Eye of the Desert, who had triumphed over dire adversities in order to hear the singing of the Stones.

In response to this announcement came forth the Chief of the City, a robust man of sun-browned face and clad in a plain white costume.

He saluted Ali then he asked, *"Whereforth cometh these tumultuous throngs with the quiet hour of this peaceful, ancient town? And by what authority?"*

"By the authority of the exalted Sibyl of the Stones. She hath aroused my soul to find the Stones that Sing that I may be filled with the wisdom and the perfume of

their song. When apprised of my desire and my quest these throngs have followed of their own accord."

"Well said and worthily. What ye seek is here. Ye are not many paces from the stones right now. I shall ask the High Priest of the Singing Stones put questions to thee."

He stepped aside and forth came the priest, a tall, slim man with shaven head and snow white garb and sandaled feet.

Questioned he, *"Who hath set thee on this journey to the rim of the earth?"*

"The Sultan of Dreams."

"Meseemeth that a decree of Fate hath sent thee. Our prophets have foretold the coming of a noble hero who in this shrine would be baptized with the virtue of the Sun, and who would revive in this long-neglected shrine the pieties and the venerations of the supreme One-All as they were chanted here in ages agone. Thou art the man. Thou art he who will rebuild the Temple of the Sun, the everliving, evergiving fountain head of the life of the World. Thou art the man. Tomorrow thou shalt be ordained and anointed as a Child of the Sun."

This awoke applause from all the crowd and a chorus of young men with the Priest broke into the chant of an ancient hymn to the Disk of the Sun. While the members of the caravan were being allotted to their habitations for the night, the Priest of the Stones guided Ali to the summit of hillock close at hand and pointing westward he said, *"Seest thou those two great pillars posed in regal purple against the golden flow of sunset?"*

"I see two solitary shafts of stone."

"At each sunrise these pillars sing as they have done for a score of centuries. At tomorrow's dawn we lead thee with us to hear the voice of the Stones that Sing."

On the morrow, in the hour before the dawn, a long parade of men, drawn up in double file, proceeded towards the lofty Stones. The Priest, accompanied by his chorus and his torch bearers, led the van. Ali and his comrades followed. The procession led through a lane flanked on both sides with pedestals from which heroic statues had crumbled long ago. Some of the pedestals still bore trunkless legs and in one place lay a great stone face half smothered in the sand.

At the end of the alley they came face to face with two colossal monolithic statues seated with hands extended upon the knees and facing the eastern horizon. The torches of the vanguard lit up the features of the great stone faces which portrayed a smile, beatific and divine, as though they knew the Great Happiness.

Athwart the east lay a band of sea-green sky which held the red lamp of Mars and the blue shine of Jupiter.

At the base of the statues the two columns of marchers parted and encircled the Statues until they met behind them. Then together they returned toward the east until they halted on a lofty ledge of rock between the stones and from which there was a view of the vast horizon. Here were lighted pots of incense and from them rose straight heavenward streams of pale vapors, the incense of the Sun.

Here the Priest and his attendant singers began the rechanting of the most ancient sacred ritual known to man, the Salutation of the Dawn:

"Harken ye! Harken ye!
to the Salutation of the Dawn.
Consider this Day.
For it is the very life of your life.
In this brief circle are all causes and all occasions
and all sanctions.
All realities of your existence,
the joy of living - the joy of action - the glory of beauty.

For yesterday is now but a dream,
and tomorrow but a hope.
But today if rightly lived, makes every yesterday
a remembered happiness
and every tomorrow a star of hope.
Consider ye this passing day
the day that is here."

The litanies of the dawn continued. The cithera were stroked to music and the plaintive flutes joined them. Louder grew all the sounds until the rim of the sun-disk peeped rosy above the rim of the desert. Then the clash of cymbals joined in with the beat of tabors. Loudly the chorus sang the ritual calling the Sun back to the world. Loud hosannas and exhortations continued until the Lord of the Day was above the rim of the sky and shedding his warmth upon the world.

Full on the great Stone faces fell the heat of the sun. Then faintly the images began to croon throughout their colossal forms. Ever louder grew this humming until it became as the voice of great organ pipes. In different keys and octaves sang the statues but always in harmony one with the other.

It was a god-like anthem whose grandeur maddened the fancies into prophesies. Into Ali's brain flamed the revelation of the life of the Sun which is poured into all living creatures of the world and he exclaimed, *"Hail Uriel! Make me a child of the Sun! Life of the World!"*

This pleased the Priest and he hastened to proclaim, *"Our prophets have foretold thy coming. Thou art a Child of the Sun. I proclaim thee Ali of the Sun."*

They poured cold water on his head. Then they anointed him with the perfume of the Sun.

The chorus applauded, *"Hail Ali of Ingdad! Henceforth thou art Ali of the Sun."*

Said the Priest, *"O Ali, hast thou heard the music of the Stones that Sing? Thou hast now the perfume of the Sun."*

"My soul hath heard. Its beauty and its wisdom are beyond words but I shall instruct my singers to express the meaning in their music."

For three days the Apollonian festivals continued in the City of the Sun. There were games and athletic sports and contests in song and with musical instruments. Ali marveled at the extensive ruins of the place, images of fallen gods, and prostrate obelisks and half buried stelae graves with forgotten hymns of the Sun. Ali promised the Apollonians he would revise these hymns and set them to a new music. One of the stelae bore the recipe of a perfume which was once sacred to the sun.

When Ali departed the town of the Apollonians hailed him as a Sultan of the Sun. Men and families of the city joined in with Ali's band bound for the Well at the World's End.

"Mother of the Gods: Source of all life: Magna Mater The Mistress of All - the All Nourisher - All Begetor -the Mighty Mother and Mother of Jesus himself. She was worshiped in the depths of virgin forests and on the tops of mountains - the Mountain Mother - Dindymene or the Idean Mother."

— *Sydney Prentice*

Chapter Ten

The Stones that See

or some leagues the caravan followed the footsteps of Tryphan along the border of the River Aeavan until they came into the precincts of the Sibyl of the Stones that See.

Here they were halted by a guardsman who asked, *"Who is this that cometh hither astride a blind ass leading a proud and pompous parade through a wilderness where no human eyes behold."*

"I am Ali, the Weaver of Dreams, bearing gifts to the Shrine of the Stones that See."

"What can be more blind than a stone?"

"Aye, and what can be more voiceless? But I, erstwhile, have stood beside the Stones that Sing. I have heard them singing to the rising sun and their music hath awakened in me a divine saying of divine wisdom. I crave now the saying of the Stones that See."

"Thou hast answered well and wisely. Order thy men to make camp in these grateful spaces. Come thou with me to the pavilion of the Chamberlain and bring with thee thine officers that he may question as to thy quest."

The pavilion was well within the city. Ali responded to

the Chamberlain, *"It is my quest to meet the renowned Sibyl of the Stones that See, and hear from her lips the music and the wisdom of the Stones that See."*

"What knowest thou of Sibyls?"

Promptly Ali related of himself and his travels and of the valor and the virtue of his men, Mouzaac, Ahga Pha and Ferrista, who were with him. And he dilated on the talents of his blind musicians and his dumb dancers.

Said the Chamberlain, *"A worthy tale is thine and well worded. But I must apprise thee that our high-priestess, Nitocris, may put to each one of you a riddle. Fail to answer and she will promptly send thee hence and perchance demand of thee a forfeit of goodly value."*

Rejoined Ali, *"We are not vain or vulgar men nor impious but let her question us. I beg that thou beseech the exalted Sibyl to hear our plea."*

"Our exalted priestess doth utter sayings only when the moon is round with fullness and when the bright star Canopus is ascendant in the heavens. This is the season of the waning moon. Therefore, thou must bide awhile among us."

Came now the evening when the moon was at fullness. The Chamberlain led Ali and his men and musicians and players to the shrine from which Nitocris would utter her inspirations. They took their way through a lordly avenue bordered on either hand by stone sphinxes posed between stately palm trees. At the end of the way was a large moon-round pool replete with lotus leaves, above which on long stems were the huge flowers folded into sleeping buds.

Just beyond the pool towered a colossal statue of stone - the body of a lioness with extended paws and with the head of a woman and between these outstretched limbs and on the body of the statue was a crypt with closed doors.

Said Ali to the Chamberlain, *"O what a divine stone face this is gazing out across the world into infinity with all-seeing and enraptured eyes. The inspired hand that graved those eyes was surely a god-guided hand."*

"Thou hast divined aright. That great stone face doth envisage the meaning of the saying of the All-Seeing Eye."

Ali and his company encircled the pool and took their stations directly in front of the chair prepared for the Sibyl. It was the twilight hour. In the peaceful sky large black bats were encircling the colossal head of the stone image. Behind the closed door of the crypt was heard the chanting of a chorus of women heralding the approach of the Sibyl of the Stones that See. The doors of carved electrum unfolded and forth marched two files of torch bearers, and some of the torches were of emerald flame and others had the brilliant blue of the sky. With the torch carriers marched young girls swinging censers which embalmed the air with the odor of the Celestial Lily. Then approached a group of dancers, lithe and lovely, veiled in transparent bluish tissues bespangled with little silver stars. In the moon-tints of the torch lights, dancing in silver sandals, they coiled through a ritual dance sacred to Pasiphae, the Light Giver, the Full Moon.

Then forth from the crypt came the exalted Sibyl diademed with a disk of gold surmounted with duplicate golden horns. With the unemotional eyes fixed on the high star Canopus she proceeded to the regal chair in front and seated herself therein. Her robe was of a clinging blue-green tissue set with silver. Her bracelets and her anklets were of gold and her necklace was of resplendent pearls. Her face was as a bit of magic moonlight glimpsed in some strangely haunted, unexpected place. Her uplifted arms silenced all the singing and the sounding and the dancing. A moment sat she thus. Far above her soared the veils of incense and the torch light touched the features of the great stone face on high with the animation of a goddess divinely isolate in exalted contemplation.

Ali was so overawed by this sight that his lips leaped from his control.

Said Ali, *"O exalted Sibyl of the Stones that See! Art thou the Moon Girl? Art thou the Celestial One whose eyes flingeth a magic of moonlight over desert stones? Art thou the Empress of Dreamland? Is this sacred pool before me the Well at the World's End?"*

"Who speakest thus to me?"

"I am Ali of the Sun, well-born under the star of Leo, befriended of the Lord Star and favored of the Love Star. My quest hath never been of worldly wealth, but wealth hath sought me of its own choice. Through the wide world I wander seeking the Moon Girl by the Well where I may hear the singing words of wisdom."

"Answer first an asking I will put to thee."

"I await thy asking."

"What is it that graspeth nothing, but which receiveth all things; that refuseth nothing, but doth not keep; that partaketh of whatever lieth around it in the world, but is never defiled; that is never full and never void; and which expresseth only truth?"

Ali gazed on the burnished gold disk above her brow then he answered, *"A mirror."*

"Thou hast said. Forsooth there is nothing in the mirror - nothing real - but everything we see is there. The mirror is the symbol of the perfect mind; the symbol of the freedom of the spirit. The whole world is a mirror into which gazeth the All-Seeing Eye."

Turning to Mouzaac, she asked, *"What manner of man art thou? And why here?"*

"I am Mouzaac, the mariner, who knoweth many a secret of many a land and who hath roamed the Disk of

the World but finding as yet no rest in soul. In my latter days I seek now divine wisdom. I am hither come to hear the divine sayings uttered by the exalted Sibyl of the Stones that See."

"If thou knowest all the lands tell me what thing doth flourish undisturbed and undefiled amidst a putrefaction? What doth flourish in youth and riseth up amidst death and decay?"

Mouzaac contemplated the sacred pool and answered, *"The Celestial Lily is undefiled by the slime that embraceth its roots."*

"Well said. The wide world in reality is a Lotus Land. Consider the Lotus and keep thy mind like unto its flower."

Then to Agha Pha she said, *"What manner of man art thou? And what quest is thine?"*

"I am Agha Pha, Prince of Perfume, seeking the influence of the most exalting perfumes in the world. I seek here the perfume of the Lily of the Celestial Ocean."

"Answer first my asking: Tell me the name of the most exalting perfume and the most enduring."

"The Perfume of a Mother's Love. It hath greeted me in the grotto of the Sibyl of the Stone of Silence - the perfume of the Great Mother of Mothers - the Mother of the gods and of men."

"Well answered. That perfume is one of the Sacred Seven and among those Seven is the perfume of the Lily of the Celestial Ocean. Divine Wisdom is imparted not only by inspired music, but also by divine perfumes."

To Ferista she said, *"Who art thou?"*

"I am called Ferista the Fag, a recorder of such events as befall my worthy Ali and his comrades. May I have the honor of inscribing in my history the saying of the Stones that See?"

"Let me ask thee: What are the worthiest words ever recorded by a scribe?"

"The words of the Master: 'Thy will be done.'"

"Amen. Thou hast recorded worthily of worthy men, but of thine own self hast recorded nothing. Thou hast tended the vines of the great and powerful but thine own vineyard hast thou left unpruned. Of thyself shall be a story to rival all the tales thou has jotted of the worthy and the wise."

Then to the musicians she spoke, *"What seek these men of blindness here?"*

At a signal from their leader all the musicians responded in poetic diction sung to instrumental music which in substance was somewhat of this mind:

> ***Our eyes are stones - our good eyes were made unseeing and our light hearts were made heavy with a sweet anguish by the wiles of Gloriande of the Island of the Moon. O may the Stones that See remove the stone from every eyeball and from every heart that once more we may find our way among the honest quiet-hearted crowd of this good, lovely world.***

"Answer me and tell me now what is the wisdom of the unseeing eye?"

Said the leader, *"The unseen is the reality of the sun. The unseen is the truth which is not tricked out in some masquerade to fool the seeing eye. The unseen lieth out of space and out of time."*

"Thy blindness hath taught thee wisdom. For the visible is but the shadow of the invisible. Divine wisdom is neither to be seen by man nor to be grasped by man. It answereth to exalted music and divine perfumes."

Then asked Nitocris, *"Who are these voiceless actors? And what truth of life can they express through silent gestures?"*

Straightway, at a signal from the master, these actors

in a pantomimic dance, rendered their anguished longings with rhythmic motions accompanied by censers which exhaled appropriate perfumes. They signaled that these ears and throats had been changed into stone by the wiles of Gloriande, and they besought deliverance from the spell.

Well pleased was Nitocris and she said, *"Ye shall have hearing and song. The Divine Spirit worketh in silence and containeth all works and wonders, all perfumes and all taste. It enfoldeth the whole universe in its silence and loveth it all."*

Then the Sibyl commanded her attendants, *"Bring forth from the sacred pool some of the black ooze that lieth close upon the roots of the lotus and anoint the eyes of these musicians, and into the ears and mouths of these actors drop the fragrant liquor of the Lily of the Celestial Ocean."*

While these commands were being fulfilled the Sibyl, with half-dropped eyelids, passed into a trance. Then with upturned face and outstretched arms she repeated in monotone, *"My eye and God's eye is one eye and one sight and one knowledge and one love."*

While she continued speaking thus, there were antiphonals from her own singers. She finished. The musicians bathed from their eyes the black anointment and they saw. Then the silent actors received their hearing and in their restored voices sang a song of deliverance from evil.

Nitocris then rose up and proclaimed, *"In the beginning there was light. The Great Spirit, the One-All is light and life and mind and truth. It filleth the vastitude of all space and the beginning and the end of all Time."*

Chapter Eleven

The Tranformation

hen the caravan left the Oracle of the Stones that See many dwellers of that place joined the journeymen. They followed along the margin of the River of Heaven set with water flowers and goodly trees and through many a town and village whose dwellers wondered at this long equipage. Many young men joined the band, and other men with their families decided to risk the danger of the journey which would lead them to a new and happier home. And there were old warriors who followed when they heard this crowd was headed for a magic city with a fountain to make all old people young again.

From the peaceful river margins they turned into drouth-bitten lands which grew harsh and harsher as they went along. Then for a number of leagues they followed the pebbled bed of a wady which finally led to the very base of a mountain wall heaven-high, precipitous, unriven, bare of verdure, capped with snow and of aspect most forbidding. One of the highest peaks spat forth flame and smoke. At the base of this awful uplift the journeymen came to halt - there seemed to be no farther on.

Said Mouzaac, *"This must be the great wall that is said to rim the limits of the world."*

"Then the Well must surely be close at hand," answered Ali.

"This is the end of a fool's errand," Ferista added.

They looked upon a savage landscape far and wide. No living thing was here. The sun was sinking just beyond the forbidding wall and sable shadows crept forth like the fingers of the evil genius of the land.

Dark forebodings and bitter doubts disturbed the crusaders. They became a maddened mob and from them came such cries as these, *"We are led astray by a mad man on a blind-eyed ass. We have no food or drink."*

"Ali, slay the camels and the dogs for this our last repast on earth."

"Death to the fool who hath beguiled us to this stony sepulchre."

Some with the laughter of a maniac shrilled, *"Well at the World's End! Magic City! The last act of a farce of a fool! And we have been the actors in this farce! Ah ha! Ha! ha! ha! All Hell will shake with laughter at our doom! See how yonder mountain spits forth the fire-breath of Hell - the laughing lavas of the infernal world!"*

"Be not discouraged at what ye see," proclaimed Ali. *"We are indeed at the World's End and the Well is but a little farther on. Abide here in the peace of hope and confidence until the morn. I go to spend the night beside the Well. At sunrise I shall return and announce the gladsome news!"*

Mouzaac proclaimed, *"Be of heroic hearts. Behold the epic aspect of the landscape! Behold those two mighty mountain pinnacles. One is capped with ever-lasting ice and the other breathes forth eternal rubescent fires. They are the Horns of the World, famous in fable and song - the Horn of Ice and the Horn of Fire! The*

Horns of the World and the Well of the World are neighbors. All the soothsayers have told me so."

Then Agha Pha said, *"Is not this air pervaded with an incense new and strange? Is there not a music in the rumblings of the earth around us? A mighty music shakes the perfumed air around us - a cosmic symphony."*

"Brave Prince of Perfume tarry here with my Band and my actors that they may note these world-reverberations, this anthem of the Horns of the World. The night cometh on. With Ferista and Tryphan I shall press on yet a little farther to the Well. On the morrow I shall return with a new song for this poor incredulous over-anxious crowd."

Ali and Ferista and the blind white ass Tryphan went out into the swift-gathering gloom to discover what yet might be found at the end of the trail.

Night's mantle brought no blackness because the torch of the fire horn lent the dusty desolation an unearthly glow. The rumblings and the tremblings of the world became more frequent. Around this desolation the capricious winds rebuffed from all directions and many a sportive spiral of dust played in the gales.

Of a sudden they found themselves astray in a mass of pallid ruins of what had once been a city great and gay. They proceeded through the ruins on a highway with a curving course like the trail of some great serpent. Along this way stood many a shrine, some of which still contained an image of a god, and some were like empty tombs. Then they came to the ruins of domed dwellings of the nobles which appeared like acres of gigantic mushrooms leaning in all attitudes. These mushroom shapes were domes of stone which once had crowned dwellings. Some of the dome-shaped lodges stood intact as though they were deserted only yesterday. All these tombs and domes and fallen walls and pillars were cast in a nitriferous encrustation crystalline and sparkling as salt and which had been spewed forth long ago by the very mountain which was now troubling the heavens with infernal fires.

Exclaimed Ferista, *"A region of Tombs. The journey of life leads but to the grave! Here we are at the end of our way, the end of our folly. Come now Ali, let us choose for our bones one of these crystalline tombs."*

"Our path leadeth beyond this section of tombs. By this blood-colored light let us see what awaits at the end of this serpentine trail," said Ali.

"Our comrades will slay us if we return to tell of this graveyard awaiting them here. I can feel death creeping over me. My feet can go no farther. I am fainting from hunger and thirst and despair. See here! This shall be my resting place. See what a beautiful tomb is this that is mine!" sighed Ferista.

Ali peered within. *"Thou art deceived. This was never built for a tomb. It was fashioned for the home of a noble. See! It hath chambers and mosaic walls and floor. And yonder is a couch of carved wood designed for pleasant napping."*

Ferista tossed his garment upon the couch and sprawled himself therein. *"Here I shall sleep. Dear Ali, may we soon meet in the after-world."*

Ali left him there and, with patient Tryphan, proceeded along the unknown way of a long-dead city.

Over the sandy serpentine trail of the wady they went until stopped by a high stairway of large stones which had once been a bed of cascading water. Ali dismounted and climbed with the beast. They came to a plaza wide and windswept, sanded and solitary and in the center stood a flat-topped pyramid from which rose veils of vapor like spirits coming forth into the night. Like a great sacrificial altar this truncated pyramid appeared, and circling round its base was a procession of wind-spirals in playful undulations. Towards these frolicsome whirling winds Tryphan tramped and Ali followed so near that the winds dallied with his hair. He detected whispered words among the breezes.

Distrust and fear beset his heart as he responded, *"O laughing singing winds! Are ye laughing now at this clown of fools, who, after long-suffering in wide-wanderings in search of a well with the waters of life, hath found himself in a region of tombs set in a dusty desolation?"*

Light laughter rippled from dust spirals of desert sand.

"Hear me, O deathless winds of the waste, happy winds with no care for food or drink, ever-wandering but never weary, wise as to all highways and all deeds of wayfaring fools, hear one and have your fill of laughter now! Have I, a credulous fool, been lured here by a treacherous Tale of a Turk only to die an obscure death?"

Louder laughter came from the winds.

Cried Ali, *"What place is this where now I am to die? And for what purpose? And for whose sport?"*

Again there was universal wind laughter and one of the Wind-whorls took on a diaphanous likeness of a young maiden gyrating in a dance with her long tresses drawn upwards like the flames of a torch. Three times she whirled around Ali.

Then in the language of the grasshoppers she spoke, *"This is the Playground of the Winds. This is the Desert of Loneliness. Here we assemble in concourse betimes for disport and delight. Hither are come the Four Winds of the World tonight with the many lesser winds, and here we murmur what we discover in all our wanderings. What tale canst thou tell to the winds?"*

"O form phantasmal! Art thou one of the thousand forms of the Moon Girl? Art thou but a lovely lure to destruction? Art thou come here to witness the burial of a deluded weaver who hoped for the Day of the Bridegroom?"

Dancing Wind-whorl

"The Moon Girl hath a thousand names. I am known as the Song of the Winds. I do wander everywhere with the wings of the winds."

This aroused wild laughter and in this merriment Ali divined the tones of the Gabalouk like unto a muffled thunder.

Cried Ali, *"O Gabalouk! Patron of all fools! Hast thou lured me through a life-long quest solely for thy delight at my folly and misfortune? Answer me!"*

"Bélhamarámara!"

Thundered the Gabalouk, *"This is the goal of thy quest. Only in the Desert of Loneliness can the seed of wisdom sprout in thy foolish mind."*

Ali's downcast eyes glimpsed a human skull half-buried in the sand. Tremblings of fear seized upon him and copiously he wept.

"Alackaday! Meseems I have set my heart upon fooleries instead of wisdom and what I have mistaken for Wine of Life was but a brew of the Gall of Death!"

At the touch of the teardrops of Ali the sands twitched like the hide of a lion stung by a gadfly and these twitching sands began to sing and croon. In wonder Ali withdrew a pace.

"Whence cometh this murmuring music? Is it from the sand or is it from that sightless skull half buried close?"

Answered the Gabalouk, *"Thy tears of contrition have awakened the desert sands to song."*

"O Gabalouk! This song to my ear is sweeter than the singing sands of Gloriande's isle!"

"Thou hearest now the sweetness of the saying which the Master once wrote upon the sand with his finger."

"O Gabalouk! I am hearing the singing sands."

"The sands remember all traceries that are ever made upon them. They remember every pretty sand castle

that has been moulded from them. Therefore do not shrink from building castles on the sands. Be like the sands. Forget not the music that is just now being traced upon thy soul."

Then all the winds made a chorus from the melody which came up from the tear-touched desert floor.

Ali called out, *"O Song of the Winds! O music of the sands that sing! Speak now thy words of judgement, O Gabalouk. Now I am not in the least afraid to die."*

"Thou shalt not die. In every fool there is a seed of virtue. Thy years of contrition and confession have sprouted a seed of wisdom in thy soul. Thou hast the virtue of steadfastness of purpose. It shall bear fruit. Speak now thy heart's desire."

"To know the Saying that Sings."

"Only the voice of the Over-Wind can tell thee that. I am but the Gabalouk, one of the Ground Winds. Only the Wind of the stars can tell."

"How may I hear that exalted voice, O Gabalouk? Tell me that and I will pledge thee all my days to thy service."

"Thy pledge doth please me. I count thee in my service. I have neither arms nor fingers. I can destroy but I cannot build. I can carve away a mountain of rock and destroy a city of stone but I cannot rebuild. So make for me here a Pleasure Dome whose topmost banners may play in the Over Wind and bring down to earth the vibrant music that is always there, the music of the Saying that Sings."

"I swear me to thy service."

"I will supply thee with all the needed tools and craftsmen."

"On my soul I vow to build the tower."

"Restore for me this long-dead city. Restore its aspect in accord with thy fancies. Build me here a festive town of faerie design: for great is my delight in fictive fancies.

And name the city Phantomah - a city of the joy of the winds; a city of magic, and thou shalt wear the title of Prince of Phantomah."

All the wind voices repeated, "Phantomah. Hail Prince of Phantomah!"

Then a wide silence fell upon the landscape. It seemed that every wind had left the place. Ali stood with eyes fixed on the half-buried skeleton at his feet.

"Am I in a dream? Have I really heard the Song of the Sands repeated by the singing winds? Can it be that the song I have been seeking hath sought and found me here? Or were all these sounds but a tumult of my maddened mind? Am I not in the Realm of the Dead?"

Tryphan was climbing the slope of the pyramid in the center of the square. Ali followed after. In the center of the platform of the pyramid top was the mouth of a crater half the measure of a man in height and more than the measure of a man across. It was a vent of vapors, an orifice in the earth, which in past ages had blubbered up through volcanic plasmas which had hardened round the rim. Ali peered into the depths of this darkness. Once more his eyes flooded tears which fell into the abyss. There was a sound of turbulence deep down. Ali withdrew and stood beside Tryphan. The turbulence in the well had the sound of rising waters.

Whispered Ali, *"Have I not heard that the Well at the World's End is fed by tears that drip in sorrowful nights? But surely this sulphurous mouth of hell cannot be the Well."*

Then appeared a monstrous sight. A raft of rotten reeds bulged up above the rim of the well. Dome-shaped it halted there and from beneath this raft trickled forth waters darker than a deep hued wine. In the center of this raft of reeds sat an aged bony woman garbed in tatters grey as the reeds.

"Mad usurper of this city of rest! Thy tears have scalded

me out of a cool, long sweet sleep. Thou hast awakened slumbering waters from the foundation of the world. Who art thou, wretched wight all tear-stained and bedraggled in a beggar's garb? Why comest to trouble the rest of this city of tombs?"

Her eyes gleamed like two coals of fire in the ashen grayness of her wrinkled face.

Resolutely Ali responded, *"I am the Prince of Phantomah duly ordained to rebuild this city and to raise here a pleasure-dome whose banners shall flutter in the highest wind and bring down harmonies of the Winds of the Sky."*

"Presumptuous imposter! Prince of Phantomah! Ah ha! ha! Ragged rogue! Rider of a blind jackass. Ha! ha! ha! Who hath dubbed thee Prince of Phantomah? Be it that blind ass of thine?"

"The mighty Wind god, the Gabalouk, who cometh here betimes to frolic with the lesser winds. He hath instructed me in his ritual in the Cavern of the Winds. He hath ordained me to give this place the name of Phantomah."

"That Gabalouk, the giver of goodly things to a fool! But indeed the Gabalouk is no fool. All men are fools - even those men who think themselves wise. But, presumptuous Prince, what seekest thou here?"

"The Well at the World's End which is the fountain of the Wisdom that Sings. The Well where dwelleth the Moon Girl who flingeth a glory over a wasted land. And where groweth the Tree of Knowledge - the World Tree."

She laughed and laughed and laughed again.

"O far-wandering fool, life-journeying on a blind ass, bound for the Well at the World's End. Ah ha! ha! ha! Oh hee, hee! This is the Center of the World! This is the navel of the Earth. Let me stay this laughter ere I wake the dead around us here."

Anger overpowered the chagrin of Ali. He exclaimed, *"Hag of Hell! Thou art ugly as the words that thou hast uttered!"*

"Disparage not my speech, young man. I speak the truth, and truth is sometimes ugly to vainglorious souls."

"Hath some sorcery conjured thee up from the mud of a noxious well to mock me only for the sport of treacherous winds? What incubus art thou? I sought the Well at the End of the World. Have I been tricked by the winds to the Center of the World?"

"It is easy to trick a credulous fool. But forsooth methinks thou has tricked thyself, Prince of Phantomah! Well do I know this city here. Many a maddened-minded hero hath tried here to build a tower to the sky, but every tower hath tumbled in its time. On every hand behold the ruins of these endeavors, and every time a tower fell the city died. Why art thou constrained to build where other fools have failed?"

Ali stood tooth-chattering as with a chill while he contemplated fallen towers all around him.

Urgently the dark-hued waters pushed the raft of dead reeds upwards until it sloughed off from the orifice and lodged on the edge of the pyramid. The withered witch remained seated in the center of the mat and she kept beating her bony arms in the spuming flood which divided around her and cascaded down the pyramid. Now and then a bird darted from the well, shook its wings and body and circled overhead. And at times a lotus bud was in the flood and strange fruits and vines, and finally came green branches laden with figs or pomegranates or apples. Then the woman stood upright in the force of the flood which tore away her tattered garb and reclothed her with strands of verdure and with the girdle of a grapevine around her waist. She shook the water from her heavy locks and promptly the winds wafted them upwards. She walked from the water and stood upon dry ground, a lovely youngish figure to behold. With dainty feet she pirouetted on the sands while swinging a strand of fragrant grapevine as she danced.

Then turning a smiling face to Ali she called, *"Am I a Hag of Hell?"*

"Thou wonder of witchery! Thou art lovely to the eye as is the new moon seen all unexpected after a day of storms. Bright transfiguration! Teller of Truth! Is there food enough and drink enough in Phantomah to feed my hungry hosts all the year? Mine army waiteth now just outside the city."

"Hast not thou read how a prophet of old brought forth living waters from a smitten stone? Hast not thou read how the Bread of Heaven fell by night on desert stones? What hath happened doth happen and will happen. Search the stones around this place at daybreak and gather the manna that awaits thee there."

"O miraculous maiden! Art thou the Moon Girl? Tell me what thy lovely name is."

"She hath a thousand names."

"What name is thine?"

"Veritania."

She swung the grapevines closer to her. Again she whirled and pirouetted on the sands, swinging the vines in graceful curves. The blossoms on the vine gave forth a perfume that embalmed all the sandy desolation.

Then little whirlwinds came and waltzed with her - faster and faster in a whirling dance - then up and away in the sky she went.

By now the Morning Star was high above the rim of the world and the horns of the returning sun were upflung in the east. Ali outran the flow of the flood through the wady and came to the lodge where Ferista was sleeping.

"Awake! Awake! A new day is at hand!"

"Am I dreaming? Or are we dead? Is this a resurrection and is this our awakening in the afterworld?"

"Awake Ferista!"

"Oh, I had a dreadful dream last night! You and I were dying of hunger and thirst and...."

"Quench the memory thereof! While I am speaking there is a stream of water bearing fruits and blossoms and flowing past the door-sill of this thy chosen tomb. During thy dream of famine a mouthful of manna hath fallen upon the city of thy tomb."

"O Ali! Where hast thou been all this night? Thou bearest the odor of the flowers of the grapevine!"

"It is the perfume of the vine that clings to the World Tree."

"Wherefore that look of gladness in thine eyes?"

"O Ferista! The well I sought hath sought and found me here. And in my most sorrowful night I have heard the melody of the Sands that Sing."

"But what of the singing sands of the isle of Gloriande?"

"The songs of the Moon Isle were but for a fool's delight."

"And what of the World Tree whose roots drink of the Well?"

"Garlands from that tree laden with apples are being tossed from the spring atop yonder pyramid. Look and believe thine eyes!"

"Ah let me bathe in this river, and slay my hunger."

"Hasten to the camp Ferista! We must outrun these waters ere they be the first to herald the glad news that a feast is prepared in the wilderness."

They set forth together with Tryphan between them laden with branches of apples and pomegranates.

*"The all-working, all wishing, all-smelling,
all-tasting one, that embraceth the universe,
that is silent, untroubled that is my Spirit
within my heart: that is Brahman."*

*"There is a spirit that is mind and life, light
and truth and vast spaces - that contains
all works and desires and all perfumes and all tastes."*

*"Nothing happens by chance, but everything
through a cause and of necessity."*

*"I am the Light of the sun and the Moon;
beyond the darkness I am the brightness, the rays
of everything that shines. Sound in the ether,
perfume on the earth, the eternal seed of all that
exists, the life of everything. As wisdom I live in
the hearts of all."*

— Bhagavad Gita

Chapter Twelve

Ali Builds the Magical City

n brief season the city of Phantomah was much recovered from its ruins, and the whole course of the wady leading from the town became a stream of living water. The report of the miraculous place went out far and wide and long caravans of people came to make their dwellings here.

Among the throngs were warriors and artisans and builders with their wives and children and slaves. All along the course of the wady banks of verdure sprouted and many an old abandoned farm became bountiful with harvests, and herds and flocks of fowls.

To all these bands of immigrants the Chaplains of Ali said, *"We welcome thy coming to Phantomah. Make thy home with us and help us build the loveliest city of the world."*

Ali reconstructed many a desecrated shrine and he consecrated them to the mysteries of the Seven-fold secret of celestial things. There was a shrine to Uriel, the Soul of the Sun, and a shrine to the veiled Goddess whose emblem was the moon round whose Spirit was Pasiphae; and a shrine to the Magna Mater which is the Earth Star; and one to the Love Star, Mistress of the Dawn and the Dusk, and a shrine to the Lord Star who rideth the winds and flingeth the thunderbolts. And there was a shrine to the World Tree, the emblem of knowledge and the emblem of earth and heaven. Not least among the sacred chapels was one called The House of the Lion, sacred to the Stars of Leo.

Phantomah prospered as by magic. It grew like the mushrooms of the fays that wax in night shades. The city became beautiful with domes and slender towers that tapered at the tips like buds of roses, and all of them were brightsome with flickers of silver and gold.

Some of the domes were like the moon, when half-risen on the desert's rim, and some were bulbous and crowned with crescents. Some had the mellow curves of melons.

The Avenue of Shrines led to a street of stately colonnades and serpentined under high-flung arches here and there. The facades of Phantomah were like silent melodies, and there were garden plots and verdant parterres like bits of Paradise.

But chief of all the wonder-works in this wonder-town was the Pleasure Dome which Ali built in homage to the winds. He called this dome the Bowl of Heaven. High among the towers of the town it was. The underside was frescoed with the twelve signs of Heaven. Like a summer cloud this inverted bowl seemed to be flying in the air. Indeed, it seemed striving to rise even higher, but cables from the rim bound the dome to the earth. All around the rim hung ball-shaped bells which made a mellow harmony when tossed by the winds.

Inside this dome hung clusters of bronze shields and

swords and lances gathered from historic fields of battle, and all these pendulous metals chimed when the Bowl of Heaven swayed in the tides of wind.

A mechanistic miracle it was. By night no eyes could tell what held that dome in air, but a daylight gaze might disclose this dome upheld by mighty kites flying high in the Over Wind. Some of these kites were so very high that scarcely were they seen, and from each kite a banner trailed.

It was a worthy tribute to the wishes of the Gabalouk which Ali had sworn to fulfill. All who came to Phantomah marveled at this murmuring Bowl of Heaven kite-hung in the sky, not knowing that the music in that bowl came down on the vibrating cords that rose up to the kites high in the Over Wind. In the never varying, never shifting Wind of the Sky - Wind of the Stars, this dome was ever singing the Music of the Spheres.

All the people of the city hailed Ali as Prince of Phantomah, and the Keepers of the shrines hailed him as Ali of the Sun. The fame of Phantomah brought hither pilgrims of divers demeanors all curious to behold the wonders within the walls that now bound the town. So it became expedient to question and inspect each new arrival and to exclude all inauspicious men. For this office Ali appointed Ferista as Keeper of the Gate and he appointed Agha Pha as Wazir of Perfumes that he might, at the gate, ward off the entry of any ill-odorous baggage which might offend the city which bore the gentle perfumes of the grapevine. Mouzaac was made a Wazir-warden whose duty was to ward off fugitive thieves and revengeful assassins and ill-natured rabble-rousers who plant seeds of discontent among the peaceful.

These three men were on a day together in a chamber behind the grille beside the gate when appeared outside a sinister old man trudging afoot, swarthy, bearded, tousle-haired and clad in a wrinkled suit of leather. His shoulders bore the knapsack of an itinerant peddler. His eyes were black and piercing, his fingers long and claw-like, and his haughty smile disclosed two rows of hard white teeth.

"What man art thou?" called Ferista. *"And wherefore cometh?"*

"Only the Prince of Phantomah shall hear my name, and only the Prince shall know my errand. Inform his Highness that to his gate hath come a vendor of the rarest of rareties with a lamp to illumine the mind and a perfume to ennoble the soul and which endureth even to the gates of Paradise."

"What manner of knave be this who demandeth, with no beseeching, an audience with Prince Ali?" said Ferista.

"Methinks he stinketh like a stable," said Agha Pha.

Rejoined Mouzaac, *"His ill-bred tongue would jar the palace. He is perhaps a rogue."*

"Thou beggarly bunch of rags! Thou insolent, ill-smelling, ill-bred fellow! We will have none of thee! Begone!" declared Ferista.

"Smug keepers of this gate advise your Sultan that I will put before his eyes gems to cheapen all his hoard. Tell him I have for his ears a tale to make him bow his head to my feet. What matter robes? What matter rags? I bring to your Sultan what will cheapen all his robes. I heard your churlish words that I outstink a stable! Ah, ha! ha! In my knapsack I have a vial to surpass all other fragrances - a perfume which endureth all life long - which doth penetrate not only flesh and bone but also the very soul.

"I heard you fellows say my speech might jar the Sultan's ears. Inform him that of late I have spoken with high potentates of the world, parried speech on their

own exalted level. Tell your Sultan I have a penetrating tale for him."

"Thou hast the babble of bibacity! Get thee gone!"

They slammed the door in his face.

On the morrow that same peddler was still there, impudent, imperious and voluble in fast discourse. A second time Ferista denied him entrance.

When on the third day this same man was at the gate and with his same trenchant monologues, Ferista himself hurried to Ali to report, *"A saucy wight unpleasing to the eye persisteth now a third day at the gate, demanding, not requesting, an audience with thee. This ragamuffin said he hath lately parried worthy speech with princes in their palaces. He smelleth like a wild beast yet he said he peddles perfumes which endure all life long - aye which endure in the soul even to the gate of Paradise. So he said. He hath the swagger of a taproom, yet he hath dined in the halls of lordly men. So he said. He hath been world-wide in wanderings and is known in every palace. So he said. He cometh now to thee."*

Said Ali, *"Show the saucy beggar through our city. Show him our avenues, shrines and temples, and our never failing fountains and our Bowl of Heaven floating in the air. Then bring this churl to me. Perhaps the knave may act out some role of merriment in my hall. I am somewhat weary of the proud and puffed-up fellows overdressed in lavish gowns and smelling of pride and self esteem. .In my Hall of State I shall parry with the saucy jester. It may be that we'll trick him out in cap and bells. E'en though he smelleth like a hostler we shall send him forth well ordered and well adorned. I am in a mood just now for quips and quirks. So show the ragged rascal in."*

Ferista hurried toward the gate only to meet the stranger approaching in the avenue. *"How comest thou hither without authority?"*

"I have my way of entry into any unwilling town. I am my own authority. Here am I on my way to the Sultan's palace."

With fear and suspicion Ferista guided the peddler 'round the city and then delivered him to the palace door.

Meanwhile Ali had put on splendid robes and a great turban bejeweled with rubies and emeralds and peridots and pearls. His slippers were jeweled and turned up at the toes. He awaited the stranger in the sumptuous ante chamber to which he gave the name of Alcove of Weavings and which was hung with tall tapestries from the ceiling to the tufted carpet on the floor. Here were fuming censers and caged birds of rare plumage, and carved ivories and jades, and beside the golden chair of Ali a large tame leopard lolled.

In came the man. He kicked off his dusty shoes and in bare feet strode nonchalantly through the elegance around him. In no sense was he over-awed. He triffled with the tufted trappings, sniffed the censers, toyed with the bird cages, and he looked the snarling leopard directly in the eye. In front of the chair of Ali he dropped his leather knapsack to the floor. He saluted and salaamed in oriental style and then with folded arms he stood waiting word of the Prince of Phantomah.

"What fool cometh here? And why? And whence? And whither bound? And who hath sent the fool to me?"

"The Sultan of Dreams hath directed me here. I am but a journeyman vendor. Therefore I shrink from declaring my plebeian name to one who beareth the title of Prince of Phantomah. I dwell in no place because I am always world-wandering. I am bound for the Well at the World's End."

"Ah, ha, ha! Now I know thou art a fool, for this is the

Center of the World. And what could be farther from the center than the rim?"

"By those words, O Prince, I know thou art the fool, not I. The Well at the Center and the Well at the rim of the world! It is my turn to laugh. A ha! I have a tale of those wells which can make thee confess thyself to be the dupe of fools."

How white and hard his heavy teeth gleamed forth.

"I care naught for any tale of thine, saucy peddler. Make brief the wherefore of thy visit for I have affairs of state which await my ears and my judgement."

"Let thy stately affairs hold to silence for a spell. I have somewhat more stately and important to declare."

"What care I for any peddler's poof! My deeds speak for themselves. Have I not made a desert fountainous? Have I not established groves of fig and olive and pomegranate? Have I not built a splendid city with its Lake of Remembrance? Have I not devised a fabulous pleasure dome and hung it in the winds? Have I not brought hither all incense and perfume and spiceries of the world? Do I not possess rare gems and jewels? I was once a poor weaver of Ingdad ridiculed and rejected by the haughty and the high. Now I am Prince of Phantomah. Is that not a tale how I – a starveling boy – gained all these goodly things?"

"Truly, I have marveled at thy fictive city. I commend its sights and sounds, and savors. But chief of all its wonders I find most worthy is that Pleasure Dome in air. Thy city is a miracle to the eyes. But there is a boastful booming in thy tale. Methinks thou art purblinded by self-pride. Thou art taking credit for the whimsies of the winds. By slender cords that Bowl of Heaven hangeth on the will of the winds. By the will of the Gabalouk a single fountain feeds the many gardens of this thy rainless city. While seeking the Well at the World's End thou

hast stumbled into the happy Center of the World. Methinks that humility and gratitude should replace thy pride and arrogance. Have not unexpected guides and guards appeared along thy fool-fancied way? Have not beneficent powers been marching all the night to be thy glad surprise at sunrise? Didst you not find a ship prepared to deliver thee from the Cave of Dangers? Even these luxuries all around us here – even that sumptuous chair wherein thou resteth – have they not been bestowed upon thee? And thou! Of thyself thou didst what? What? What?"

"Thou art a peddler. I am a Prince. Make brief show of thy wares and bring prompt closure to thy parable, for I have affairs of State anon."

"So be it. Let me first display a lamp whose flame doth verify what is genuine and what is counterfeit. Whether it be a coin, a gem or a letter of love. In the light of this lamp real gems shine with greater brilliance, and false stones become as charcoal to the eye, and any falsely inscribed story doth promptly vanish from its paper. Come now! For a proof, suppose we test this lamp upon those gems set in thy turban."

"I do not give a rap for thine appraisals or for thy bothersome, boresome gabbling tale."

With averted eyes Ali rose from his chair and strode a few paces away. The leopard growled with open maw and paced the room with his master. They paced the width of the room while the vendor of lamps calmly lighted his wick and then called out, *"Prince of Phantomah! Behold thyself in the light of truth."*

When Ali returned his eyes to the man he saw depending from the vendor's swarthy finger a chain-hung lamp of beryl carved with a curve of the new moon with two all-seeing eyes on the sides and inlaid with emerald and lapis lazuli. From the center of this lamp gleamed a two-tongued flame steady as the forked fire of the planet Venus.

To himself aside Ali said, *"By all the gods where have I seen this lamp before?"*

Its light touched the turban of Ali and every jewel but one turned to jet, and that one gem was the central pearl which shone like a pearl of great price.

The vendor smiled at Ali's discomfiture and spoke, *"I find that many a prince and princess of this world are tricked out with much make-believe, and they tell much of themselves which is but a puff of fiction. The tales I tell are true."*

"Thy lamp is a clever artifice of trickery. My palace is well fitted with lamps of every land. There is in the world no lamp that can bewilder my sight."

"Hast heard of the seven branched lamp of Leonorina of Ingdad?"

These words were daggers to Ali. He dropped into his chair. The leopard snarled with yawning jaws.

"Peddler or sorcerer! What knowest thou of Leonorina and of Ingdad?"

"It is indeed an engaging tale to tell."

"Tell what thou knowest."

"But since thou hast no time for tales it behoveth me to depart."

"Friend or fiend! Comest thou here to drop coals of fire upon my heart? Thou shalt know now nothing more from me, Avant! Thou art unseemly to my sight. Thy loutish coat hath the odor of a hostler."

"As a friend I come – and as a true, kind friend. This coat of mine is cut from an old wine skin that still holds the savor of the noble wine that was first poured into it. This that thou callest a stink is really a basic aroma from which the most enduring perfumes have been blended.

Thou hast much to learn of perfumes and much to learn of perfumed wine skins."

From his coat he plucked forth an alabaster vial and upholding it, he said, *"I hold here the Perfume of the Wine Skin whose essence is the most enduring in the world. Worthy Prince, before I take my leave I challenge thee to a tournament of odors. Match the virtue of my cherished odor in its sweetness and endurance and I shall forfeit my lamp of truth to thee. And shouldst thou fail, then permit me to pluck from thy gadgets such as may please my fancy."*

"Thou hast tricked me with a lamp; think not to drug me with an odor."

Perturbed with indecision Ali rose and paced the carpet for awhile. The leopard marched beside him. Then he turned and spoke in anguished speech, *"Persistent peddler! I accept thy challenge!"*

He thrust his hand beneath his inner garment and from over his heart brought forth the vial which he had recovered from the sands where Leonorina had been bathing on her birthnight. He unclasped the vial and waved it to and fro saying, *"Here is the fragrance to challenge thine in essence and endurance. Name for me this fragrance if thou canst!"*

Said the man, *"It is the fragrance of the soul's First Love. Noble Prince, thou hast outmatched me. My lamp is thine. Thou hast perfume which will follow thee even to the gates of Paradise. Thou wearest the perfume of thy First Love. Incoherent Prince, the foundation of thine odor is very much as mine."*

Forthwith the man unstoppered the vial he held and forth came an incense which penetrated all the chamber and extinguished every burning censer. The leopard lay down at the vendor's feet.

Said Ali softly, *"Thou hast subdued my spotted beast.*

Thou hast soothed my soul. What is the perfume's name?"

"First tell me: Am I fiend or friend?"

"Thou art no foe."

"Am I kind or cruel?"

"Thy cruelty is mayhap a kindness."

"Well, this is the perfume of a kind word dropped into a lonely and pitiful soul. I call it the perfume of the Wine Skin."

"Am I a lonely and pitiful soul? Like thyself I have had my sorrow."

He made as though to depart. Ali protested. *"Stay awhile I pray thee. Thou hast a tale to tell."*

"Nay, noble Prince, thou hast affairs of state that call thee now."

"Thou hast outcalled all calls. Be my guest here in my palace until the morrow; and all the morrows shall be thine for telling!"

"Thou art a Prince. I am a peddler. For me to hear is to obey."

"But tell me, worthy wanderer, peddler of truth, blender of perfumes, tell me what thy name is. Art thou a brother of the nymph called Veritania?"

"I am, indeed, somewhat of her tribe. Well do I know Veritania. But the innkeepers of the world know me by the name of Kasan the lampman, and a vendor of fragrant lamp oils. But I have another name which is the sweetness of all sadness, a name which being interpreted meaneth Misfortune."

"Kasan of the lamp thou art my guest."

"Beneficent Prince! Accept this wine skin coat of mine. Hang it in thy most secret closet and learn the excellence of its ever-during perfume."

"Kind Kasan, tomorrow thou shalt choose from my wardrobe any garment which may please thee."

On the morrow Ali, in the plain garb of a weaver, waited in his Hall of Mirrors to receive the lamp man. It was a stately hall with mirrors overhead and on all the walls. One end of the hall was thrown open to give full view of the noble landscape with the heaven-high ice-capped mountain which was one of the Horns of the World. Facing this open end Ali was seated on a plain tabouret.

He called out, *"Let the teller of tales appear."*

Straightway two attendants led in the man. They had barbered his hair and his beard and garbed him in the regalia of a Turk and crowned him with a jeweled turban inwoven with red gold and set with pearls and gems. They flung a rug upon the floor upon which the man sat down and crossed his legs in oriental pose. Then they brought in the lamp of truth and lighted it and placed it beside the man. All the mirrored walls and ceilings displayed Turks, Turks, Turks.

"Kasan, I await thy tale."

"Ply me with questions and I shall answer. If either of us speak falsely this lamp shall shut its flaming eye. What is the first question?"

"Where lieth the Well at the World's End?"

"Directly before thine eyes. It lieth high up in the ice-mantled mountain which I see reflected in the mirror behind thee but which thou beholdest before thy face."

"But how can the World's End be so near to Phantomah which is the World's Center?"

"The Old Man up in yonder mountain can explain all those things. I can lead thee to his lodge at thy pleasure if thou so sayest."

"What knoweth thou of the lamp stand of Leonorina?"

"It hath seven branches each with seven lamps. By the magic of those seven times seven fires she hath made herself Empress of Ingdad."

"She! Leonorina! Empress of Ingdad? I cannot not believe it! Crafty Turk! Thou hast lied!"

Immediately the lamp went out.

"By calling me a liar thou hast lied. The lamp hath so declared. Recant thy lie that I might proceed."

By a flourish of his hand Ali signaled his recantation. Promptly the forked flame revived. Then said he, *"Tell me of the Empress of Ingdad."*

"She hath proclaimed a Tournament of Tales to take place in her palace at the coming of the next new moon. She hath heralded this report to the princes and potentates in all lands. To the prince who may out-tell all other tales she may bestow her hand and announce the Day of the Bridegroom."

"Hath the Empress of Ingdad heard of the Prince of Phantomah?"

"Never a word."

"And have I not a tale to tell?"

"Thou sayest."

"Can I, a guest of all uninvited, appear at this Tournament?"

"I myself am on my way to Ingdad as an uninvited guest even as I am come to this hall of thine."

"O Kasan, canst thou lead me to this Tournament of Tales?"

"I can lead thee thither before the birth of another new moon."

"By what miracle could I retrace my toilsome tread through the thousand leagues of danger fields to Ingdad before the next new moon?"

"That is a tale too long to tell to thine uninstructed, unexpectant mind. The Old Man of the Mountain can reveal it all to thee in a brevity of time. I go to him tomorrow. If it please thee, go with me as my guest."

Chapter Thirteen

The Well at the Center of the World

hen the morrow morned Ali and Kasan set out towards the impassable mountain walls from which rose the two Horns of the World: one a pinnacle of everlasting ice and the other a torch of eternal fire. Ali rode on the pink-eyed Tryphan shaggy and white as snow. Kasan rode a donkey black as the fuming Torch of the World. As they proceeded Kasan discoursed as to the nature of these portentous regions. Midway between the Horns and on a level with the plain was the Mouth of the Mountains, a veritable orifice of Orcus for it continually belched forth vapors and resounded with hostile rumblings. Kasan said it was called the Muzzle of Dangers.

When they were nigh unto the Peak of Ice, Kasan said, *"Behold that zone of gentle greenish hue along the lower borders of the heaven-high mantle of snow. It hath the sheen of everlasting ice, but of a truth it is not ice at all. It is a sheet of vitreous deposit underneath which flourish acres of fruits and flowers."*

"How came a zone of glass where there should be ice?"

"Aeons ago that ice peak spouted fire, as doth its brother peak today, and it dropped a blanket of dry pumice dust upon the breast of the mount. Then upon this depth of dust the crater spewed out a flood of molten quartz and silica which made a layer upon the dusty pumice and hardened into glass. Then the heart of the passionate mountain grew cold and its tongue of fire was silent forever. It became enrapt in aging snows which gleam there now. A flow of water from the snow crept below the blanket of glass and washed away the loose pumice. So today there remains a vast glass house. There groweth the fabulous World Tree to whose wide spreading branches clingeth the Grapevine of the Gods."

Commented Ali, *"A miracle before my eyes I see."*

"Nay," rejoined Kasan. *"No miracle. It is but the wondrous workings of the powers of the Earth."*

By devious paths and dangerous they climbed the mountain to where the air was icy cold and drifts of aged snow lay around them. They passed across fields of ice and snow until they came to a little oaken doorway over which lay a dome of ice and over the door was written: ***Knock and it shall be opened to thee.***

At Kasan's knock the heavy door moved open, and the men and their mounts marched into a grateful warmth of a garden with pathways bordered with gracious trees and shrubberies. Came forth a young man garbed somewhat as a monk to ask, *"Who cometh here and why?"*

Kasan replied, *"The Worthy Prince of Phantomah who seeketh the fountain of Wisdom."*

"A worthy guest on a worthy quest."

Kasan answered, *"He desireth to consult the Man of the Mountain concerning the things which trouble his soul."*

"Our wise father, Nestor, will receive him gladly. Follow to the end of this winding path. There lieth the lodge of Father Nestor. He will answer all thy askings."

They rode a long way through lush verdure under a translucent ceiling until they dismounted at the lodge of Nestor at the end of the way. It was a lodge of bulbous glass which, like a giant eye, jutted out from a promontory which looked out upon the world. A kind old man in a long white beard was this Nestor. He heard their mission and then persuaded Ali to recount the story of his life.

"A worthy quest is thine, courageous Prince. What thou seekest, the Well at the World's End, lieth in the back yard of thy lodge in Ingdad. Thou didst not drink of its waters because, as thou hast said, the cattle drank there."

"I fail to fathom the content of thy speech, O Father Nestor. How cometh it that after all my wide world wandering I am come to the Well at the Center of the World?"

He smiled and answered, *"The two Wells are one and the same in their waters. They are both fed by the Fountain of Wisdom which lieth in thy own backyard. I shall show thine eyes the Fountain of Wisdom. Follow me promptly for the daylight is already fast fading."*

They followed him to a spacious courtyard high-canopied with a dome of glass. On one side was the rock wall of the mountain from which a lusty flood of sparkling water spouted into a large pool which out-flowed through two tunnels, one on the right and the other on the left.

"This is the Fountain of Wisdom," said Nestor. *"The vent on the right leadeth to the Well at the World's End. The one on the left floweth to the Center of the World. In this way the two Wells are one."*

"This is still beyond my understanding," commented Ali.

Nestor replied, *"Return to my study. I will explain."*

Once more in the glass room, Nestor said, *"Look from that little bulbous window on thy right and tell what seeth thou?"*

"I see the whole city of Phantomah as though it lieth close at hand."

"Now look from the window on the left. What is there?"

In wonderment Ali exclaimed, *"I see the city of Ingdad as though it be quite near. The lamps of early evening are being lighted there."*

"Quite so. The two cities lie at the base of the same mountain. The waters of wisdom are divided between the two."

"Thou dost bewilder my understanding. How can the Center be so near the circumference?"

Nestor took a sheet of paper and marked the center. Then he bent the edge over til it touched the center.

"There you are. This world is not as flat as all the ancients have been telling. It is in some way built upon a curve. In thy wide wanderings thou hast gone all around the inside of this curve as a fly might crawl. Just now thou art where the edge is curved to the center."

"Still it doth daze my comprehension."

Nestor then plucked from a stalk an unopened flower-bud large as the bud of a lotus.

"Mark how the tips of these petals touch upon the center of the flower. Here the center and circumference are as one. So it is with the two wells."

Seeing a lingering doubt in Ali's eyes he explained, *"This much is true. It hath indeed been established. If one should set forth from his front door and proceed directly east he would, in due time, come to his back door from the west. Weave that knowledge into thy mind, and fret no longer over things which yet thou hast to know. Thy persevering wanderings away from Ingdad have brought thee home at last. Wander far and thou shalt arrive at thy home."*

"But how near is Ingdad to me now?"

"As near as is thy chosen town of Phantomah, found after many a moon of toilsome journey. Now go again to yonder window and tell what thou seest."

"I see the well-known streets of Ingdad displayed like some great map."

"Now put on this pair of spectacles and look again."

"Oh wondrous eye-glasses! I see my lodge in Ingdad as if within a stone's throw. But in my lodge there is no longer any lamp."

"Now put on this final pair of glasses. What now dost thou behold?"

"I see the fireflies all around my once-beloved lodge. Verily now I see the little fountain which placed the Well at the World's End in my own backyard, and farther on I see the darksome tarn behind my home and which once I held in fear, and which separated my cabin from the palace of Leonorina. Now my eyes are on the lawn of the house of Leonorina. Oh Prodigy celestial! Meseems I behold Leonorina herself strolling solitary on the lawn!"

He tore the spectacles from his eyes and to Nestor cried, *"What wizardry is there in these glasses? What trickery is this they play upon my eyes?"*

"No wizardry. They show thee truly what is there this moment. Look again."

"Leonorina! Can this be she? My Leonorina! I see thee beautiful as never before! Leonorina! I call thee."

He removed the glasses to say, *"Oh Father Nestor! Doth she hear my cry?"*

"Perhaps her soul doth really hear thee calling her. Perhaps. But look again."

"She is gazing upwards wide-eyed as though looking upon the stars – oh! As though looking directly into mine eyes. She stands on the rim of the waters from the Well at the World's End – and the water glistens and gleams with the light of the rising moon. Her face is beautiful as the super-dream in Dreamland from which it hath been fashioned. Leonorina is the Moon Girl!"

He fell in a swoon. After Nestor and Kasan had revived him he declared, *"I have entered into the very heart of dream land; I have beheld the Over-dream of the face and form of Leonorina. The circle of my life hath been completed. I am now at where I set out from."*

"Thou hast beheld the truth of life and death."

"Oh let me hasten back to Phantomah and weave into a tapestry the Over-dream I have visioned of my first and last and only loved one, my Leonorina."

"Be not hasty. Every life is long enough to fulfill its mission."

"How may I get to Ingdad?"

Spoke Kasan, *"Soon enough and easy enough Prince of Phantomah. Dost recall how, on our journey here, I pointed out the Mouth of the Mountain on the plain between the Horns of the World – that furious tunnel fuming with brimstone?"*

"I do."

"That tunnel pierceth straight through this Wall of the World and opens almost at the gates of Ingdad."

"But the deadly vapors of that hole!"

"They will all swiftly appease if water-carriers but sprinkle the tunnel floor with waters from this Well which is the waters of the Well at the World's Center and the Well at the End."

"Oh what a revelation! Well do I recall that cave in the mountain back of Ingdad. The cave that all men feared to enter because it had the breath of hell."

Continued Kasan, *"Through that tunnel pouring with*

waters of the Well thou shalt pass into Ingdad in full time to attend the Tournament of Tales in the halls of Leonorina. Meseems thy tale may find good favor."

"Oh fulfillment of a life's desire and all in one moment! O resplendent epilogue to my tale. I shall enter Ingdad in a great parade splendid with gonfalon and pennant and banner; with caparisoned camels; And with trumps and tabors and dancers and singers; and Nubian slaves carrying salvers of silver laden with the jewels and the perfumes which Leonorina hath longed for. I, the Prince of Phantomah, shall dazzle the Empress of Ingdad with my troubadours, my minstrels, my players of pantomime."

Father Nestor and Kasan sat patient while Ali enlarged upon the splendor of the return of Ali the Weaver to the streets of Ingdad.

Then Nestor smiled and said, *"Extravagant urge of a man in love. Thou hast yet to learn the story of the Lion's love for the sickle of the Moon. But spare thyself and thy comrades all such trial, all such turmoil! The heart of a maid is in nowise won by all the pomp and parade of external parures. A heart is won only by a heart. I would counsel thee to return to thy chamber in Phantomah – and promptly weave thy dream vision of the face and form of the damsel thou hast long loved in heart. Then with this bright portrait enter Ingdad on this white and wooly Tryphan of thine. Unfold to her the dream portrait thou hast woven and straightway all her entourage shall say with loud voice,* ***'Man hath not woven this beauty. Only madness could have made it.'*** *Earthly splendor could not serve thee more than this."*

Ali looked upon Tryphan and exclaimed, *"Behold the blind ass hath received his sight!"*

"For that reason the poor beast hath sought the fountain of wisdom. The waters have healed his blindness

even as they have healed the blindness of thy heart," said Nestor.

"I have found the Well at the World's End but I have not yet discovered the Philosopher's Stone."

Darkness now hung over all the world. Nestor bade his guests remain in the glass mountain until the day morrowed. Ali was all excitement and unrest. He paced the pavement and said, *"I can hardly wait the morrow. I must lay all these revelations before my comrade Ferista and my world wanderer Mouzaac and my Prince of Perfumes Agha Pha! They are all wiser than I. They shall decide whether I shall enter Ingdad with an army caparisoned, gonfaloned, trumpeting and triumphantly besieging or shall I enter on a humble white ass, beseeching?"*

"Will you seek afar off?
You will surely come back at last
in things best known to you
finding the best or as good as the best."

— Walt Whitman

Chapter Fourteen

Sam Encounters the Turk

ack in Sam's apartment, my reading of the *Tale of the Turk* came to a sudden stop. The final leaf of the story was missing. Sam pushed forward to fumble the book for the missing page.

"Gone for good! Now how am I to know how the dream-weaver triumphed over Leonorina? Stars of the Lion! I tell you, Bernie, this is worse to me than the loss of that aria of the Moon Girl which tonight you banished from my mind. That last page held the apocalypse of my life."

"Your immense imaginations!" I replied.

"You have been unrolling to me the scroll of my fate but the end of the scroll is snipped off. In the name of the Gabalouk, what shall I do?"

"That's a most wonderful and truthful story. It confirms what Will Shakespeare said, ***'We are such stuff as dreams are made on'****. That tale bursts the balloon of Byng's gas-bag letter with a bang."*

"Write the end of the tale yourself."

"By the Gabalouk I will. By the Dumptiad, I will. By

the Lion I will! This night Samuel Simpson has been tempted as was Ali the Weaver of Dreams, and like Ali, he listened more to katydids than to his Ferista. The seven-branched lamp stand of Leonorina is the seven chaptered book of Phoebe West. I shall write a seven chaptered book to dazzle her lamp stand. Well at the World's End! Moon Girl! Island of the Moon! Day of the Bridegroom! Song of the Winds. My book shall tell the meaning of them all."

"Your sublime book."

"It shall redeem my name which today is swine – trampled in the mud. And everywhere that Phoebe goes she shall hear my name repeated and see my name reprinted – Sam Simpson – Samuel Simpson. Sam!"

"Your sublime, ridiculous book!"

"It shall have a starry name."

"The Dumptiad," I offered.

"Call it the Single Step if you care – the Single Step from the ridiculous to the sublime. I promise you it will redeem my name. Tomorrow morning will be a rebirth of old Sam Simpson; it will be my birthday as well as yours."

Once more Sam searched the book. This time he came back a smiling, holding a page behind his back.

"You think I have THE page. Not so, but I found the next thing to it. It was a detached colored engraving depicting Ali of the Sun in full regalia."

"Look here Ferista! Here is a picture of my Ideal Self. Sit right there a moment and I will show you why that almost is the very costume I once wore in the play of Ali Baba."

Away he ran to Dexter's Trophy Room which was a veritable museum stuffed with curios from all lands. He returned in a gown and turban which resembled the picture: the same toggery in which he won fame as Ali Baba. Dexter had discovered this old costume in the Levant. It was of a green cloth embroidered with

threads of gold and bands of purple. The turban was of orange vermillion bejeweled with turquoise and amber. On the front of the turban was a crescent of sapphire.

Said Sam, *"My astral name is Ali, Sultan of the Sun."*

"Clothes make the man," I replied.

"Your astral name is Ferista. Your wish-word is Chimera. That's the world you love to fling at every plan I make. My wish word is to be ***Bélhamarámara."***

Sam strode to the window where his eyes caught the spell of the moonlight which tapestried the trees and carpeted the lawn and illumined the pallid blossoms which perfumed the night.

As though talking to himself he muttered, *"Night of voices! Night of visions! Night of the uncaptured Song of the Moon Girl, which it was singing to me out of those shadow mouths which had been kissed by the Moon Girl. O Night of pallid perfume! Night of prophecies! Night of one bright planetary start!"*

He appeared so like an actor in a comic opera that I smiled behind his back. Sublime Samuel! Ridiculous Sam! I left him there robed as Sultan of the Sun. Noiselessly I backed out of the room and retired to my little third floor bedroom for the night.

"I have brought thee a night story and a rarely pleasant relation, whose like none ever heard of at all."

— The Thousand Nights and One

Epilogue

Ali is the searching soul that wanders through the fires of life's experiences. The exhilarating mountain peaks and the dismal, suffocating swamps are all forms of the "refiner's fire" of transmutation.

Solve et Coagula - dissolve one form and recreate it in a new form. This is the ancient formula of the alchemist adepts who sought not the transmutation of base metals into gold, but the transmutation of the lower, human frequencies into the "Philosopher's Stone." This is the work of the soul as it raises the denser frequencies of its material manifestation and creates the lighted bridge to the highest frequency of Pure Consciousness.

> *"To him that overcometh... will I give a white stone and in that stone a new name written which no man knoweth saving he that receiveth it."*
>
> — Revelations 2:17

What is that new name? That new name is LIGHT BEING.

Ali had no need to return to his village (the material world) adorned in silken robes and jewel studded turban followed by a retinue of servers bearing worldly treasures. He had trusted his inner visions and dreams which had come from God. He returned to Ingdad splendidly radiant with shimmering, iridescent colors of a Self-realized Being. As he approached the dwelling of Leonorina the entire landscape burst into blazing white light. Seeing Ali, Leonorina emerged from her stately dwelling and instantly became transformed into diaphanous Light. As Ali approached her the two became one.

Irene Prentice Allemano
June 1998

The Seeker

Estofado by Irene Prentice Allemano

Irene Prentice Allemano

LET THERE BE LIGHT

— Gen. 1:3

YE ARE THE LIGHT OF THE WORLD

— Mat. 5:14